D0960795

MARVEL CINEMATIC UNIVERSE
PHASE THREE

MARVEL

GUARDIANS OF THE GALAXY VOL. 2

MARVEL CINEMATIC UNIVERSE
PHASE THREE

MARVEL
GUARDIANS OF THE GALAXY VOL. 2

Adapted by ALEX IRVINE
Based on the Major Motion Picture
Written and Directed by JAMES GUNN
Produced by KEVIN FEIGE, p.g.a.

LITTLE, BROWN AND COMPANY
New York   Boston

Little, Brown and Company
Hachette Book Group
1290 Avenue of the Americas, New York, NY 10104
Visit us at LBYR.com
marvelkids.com

First Edition: September 2017

Little, Brown and Company is a division of Hachette Book Group, Inc.
The Little, Brown name and logo are trademarks of Hachette Book Group, Inc.

The publisher is not responsible for websites (or their content)
that are not owned by the publisher.

Library of Congress Control Number 2017948501

ISBNs: 978-0-316-27166-0 (hardcover), 978-0-316-31425-1 (ebook)

Printed in the United States of America

LSC-C

10 9 8 7 6 5 4 3 2 1

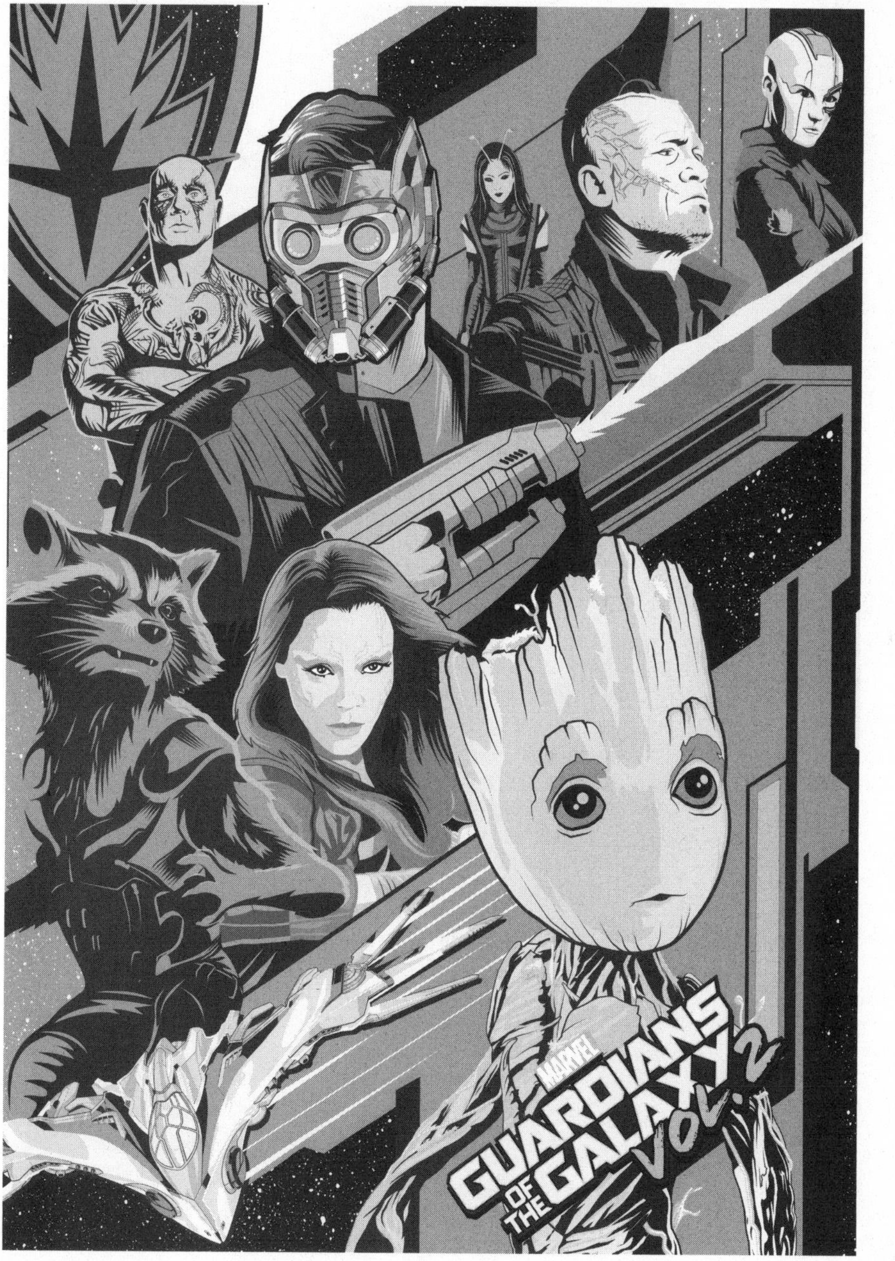
MARVEL
GUARDIANS OF THE GALAXY
VOL. 2

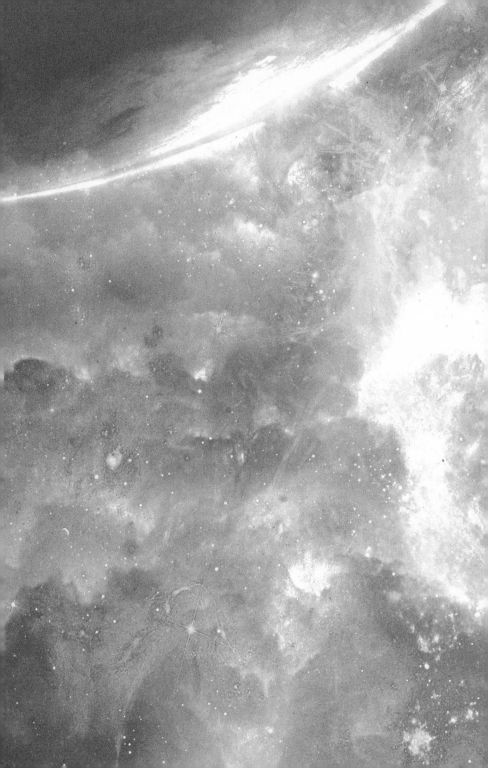

PROLOGUE

Meredith Quill had never been happier. She sat in the passenger seat of her special spaceman's convertible and laughed into the wind. He smiled at her from the driver's seat and leaned over to kiss her. The radio was playing one of her favorite songs as he sped up, racing down the stretch of Missouri country road. He'd said he had a surprise for her and she couldn't wait to find out what it was.

He slowed down and turned into the parking lot of an ice cream shop outside town. Meredith was a little surprised—he hadn't said anything about getting ice cream. But she was in love and she would do whatever he wanted to do as long as they were together. He pulled past the store and parked behind it, at the edge of the woods. Then he led her down the side of a hill to a beautiful little glade, dappled with sun that shone down through the leaves.

"Look," he said, pointing toward the ground in the middle of the glade.

A marvelous little plant grew there. It was like nothing she'd ever seen before, with spiky leaves that waved even though there was no wind. Below the leaves, the plant glowed in different colors. It seemed to brighten as Meredith's spaceman approached.

She gasped. "Oh! It's beautiful!"

"I was afraid it wouldn't take in the soil, but it grew quickly. And soon it'll be everywhere." He spread his arms, taking in everything they could see or imagine. "All across the universe."

She laughed, swept away by the grand vision. "Well, I don't know what you're talking about, but I like the way you say it."

"My heart is yours, Meredith Quill," he said.

She put her arms around his neck. "I can't believe I fell in love with a spaceman." They kissed there in the woods, with the sounds of birds around them and wind rustling in the trees. Nearby, the strange plant began to grow.

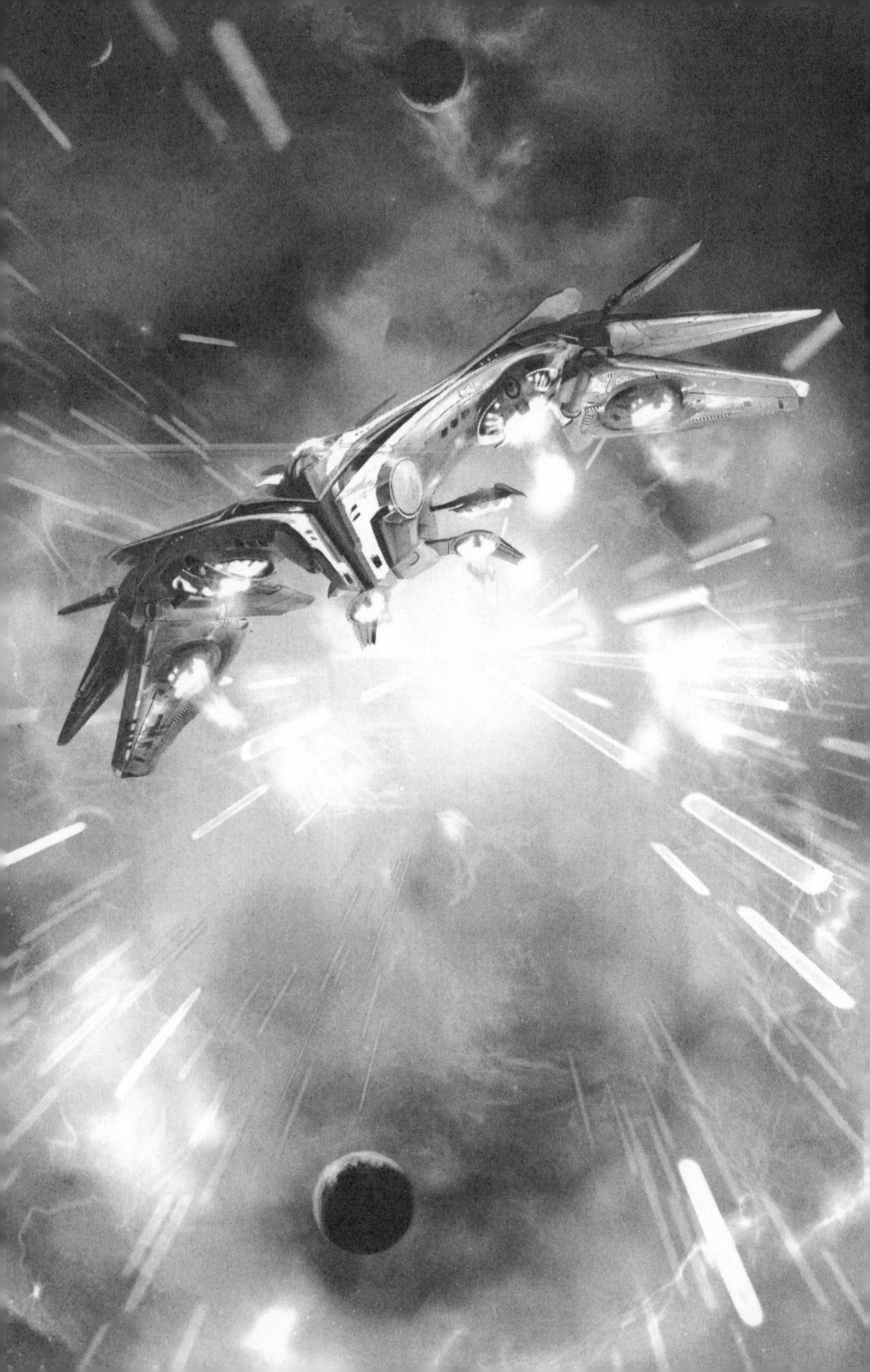

CHAPTER 1

Near the home world of the Sovereign, the Guardians of the Galaxy stood on a circular platform. Around its rim were six huge spheres that glowed with powerful energies. Closer to the center of the platform were smaller pillars that held banks of Anulax batteries, technological marvels that were also worth millions on the black market. The Guardians were there because Ayesha, the Sovereign high priestess, had learned of a threat to the batteries. She had hired the Guardians to protect them at any cost.

Peter Quill, better known as Star-Lord, looked at an old handheld video-game system in his hand. When he was a kid, he'd played endless hours of football on it. Now he had rewired it to detect the energy of the approaching threat. "Showtime, people," Star-Lord called out. "It oughta be here any minute."

"Which will be its last," Gamora said. Peter glanced over and saw she was holding an energy rifle.

"I thought your thing was a sword," he said.

She rolled her eyes. "We've been hired to stop an interdimensional beast from feeding on those batteries, and I'm going to stop it with a sword?"

"It's just that swords were your thing and guns were mine," he said. "But I guess we're both doing guns now."

She ignored him. "Drax. Why aren't you wearing Rocket's aero-rig?" The rest of the Guardians had buckled on the tight-fitting metal jetpacks. Rocket had designed them so the Guardians could all fly during combat.

But Drax, as usual, was shirtless. The dark-red tattoos covering his body seemed to ripple in the light from the glowing spheres.

"It hurts," he said.

"Hurts," she repeated in surprise. Drax was practically immune to pain.

He looked embarrassed. "I have sensitive nipples."

Rocket burst out laughing. He was busy fiddling with a machine that didn't look like any kind of weapon, but not too busy to laugh at Drax.

"What's he doing?" Drax snapped.

"I'm finishing this so we can listen to tunes while we work!"

"How is that important?"

"Blame Quill! He's the one who—"

Peter held out a hand and cut him off. "Actually, I'm with Drax on this one."

"*Ohh,*" Rocket said. He winked at Peter. "I see."

"No, seriously," Peter said. "I side with Drax."

Rocket kept winking. "I understand that. You're being very serious right now."

"I can clearly see you winking," Drax said.

"I was using my left eye?" Rocket said. He stopped winking.

Nearby, a sapling version of their formerly hulking partner, Groot, was chasing around a small group of lizard-like alien creatures called Orloni. They seemed to be everywhere throughout the galaxy. He knocked one over and shoved another away from him. Then he turned to Rocket and announced, "I am Groot."

"They were *not* looking at you funny," Rocket said.

Everyone looked up as an interdimensional wormhole opened in the sky: a huge whirlpool of multicolored energy with lightning flickering around its edges. A monstrous creature hurtled through it, as big as Quill's spaceship, the *Milano*. Its body sprouted tentacles in every direction, and its round mouth was lined with razor-sharp teeth as long as Quill's arm. It roared, shaking the platform, and dove toward the Guardians.

"That's intense," Rocket commented.

The monster crashed down on the platform, and Drax, knives out, roared right back at it. The Guardians formed up and charged at the creature. All of them but Drax and Groot took to the air using Rocket's aerorigs. They blasted away at it with their weapons, and Drax struck at it with his knives. The monster's tentacles flailed around, knocking them out of the air. It also screamed out blasts of concussive energy from its huge maw.

Very intense.

Meanwhile, Groot was looking at the stereo Rocket hadn't quite finished. He picked up two cables and tried to stick them together. After a couple of tries, he got them connected, and Peter's new favorite cassette, Awesome Mix Vol. 2, blared out over the platform. The music got Groot dancing, while the battle raged around him. A tentacle smashed down just behind him, and a moment later Star-Lord landed next to it. "Groot!" he shouted, but before he could say anything else, the tentacle slapped him away.

Groot kept on dancing, oblivious to the chaos. "Groot, get out of the way!" Gamora shouted. "You'll get hurt!"

He just heard his name and waved happily at her. She smiled back and called out, "Hi!" while still blasting away at the monster. Then she took off, and Groot danced along the edge of the platform until he was distracted by a large bug flying near his head. He chased after it, and when he caught it, he stuffed it in his mouth.

"No, no, no!" Rocket yelled, landing and slapping at the back of Groot's head. "Spit it out. Come on." Groot did, and the bug flew away. "Disgusting," Rocket growled. Then he rejoined the battle.

Without anyone watching him, Groot saw one of the

Orloni scampering by. He shot out a vine and grabbed the fin on its back, catching a ride. The Orloni ran crazily through the battle, underneath the monster and out the other side, with flames and explosions everywhere Groot looked. He lost his grip and rolled across the platform, ending up next to the stereo. The music was still pumping, so Groot started dancing again—until a few seconds later, when Drax came flying through the air and landed on the stereo, smashing it to pieces.

Furious, Groot started pounding on his back. Drax barely noticed. He got up, pieces of the stereo still stuck to his skin, and said, "The beast's hide is too thick to be pierced from the outside! I must cut through it from the inside."

Gamora, still doing her best to slow the beast, stopped. "What?!"

Laughing like he was having the time of his life, Drax charged across the platform, knives raised.

"No, no, wait, Drax!" Gamora screamed at him, but he didn't pay any attention. At a full sprint, he leaped straight into the monster's mouth. It bit down and he disappeared.

Star-Lord couldn't believe what he was seeing. He landed next to Gamora. "What is he doing?"

"He said its skin is too thick to be pierced from the outside, so he had to—"

"That doesn't make any sense!"

"I tried to tell him!"

"It's the same thickness from the inside as from the outside!"

"I realize that!"

Star-Lord thought fast as he scanned the monster. "There's a cut on its neck," he said. That was the only place they'd been able to wound it. "Rocket! Try to make it look up!"

He took off again, flying high enough to shoot down at the monster. Rocket joined him. It was working! The monster looked up, belching colorful attacks and swiping at them with its tentacles. Gamora sighted the wound and squeezed the rifle's trigger.

Nothing happened. It was empty.

"Gah," she said, and flung it away. She drew her sword and, just as Drax had, she dashed across the platform. The monster had Rocket and Star-Lord in its tentacles, but she still had a clear shot at the wound. Using one of its tentacles as a springboard, she jumped high and sank her sword into the wound. Her body weight did the rest, pulling her back down to the ground as her sword ripped the monster open in a shower of thick green goo.

She hit the ground and stepped back as the monster flailed in its death throes and collapsed with a huge boom. A moment later, Drax, covered in the green goo, slid out from the wound and raised both arms in triumph. "Yes!" he shouted. "I have single-handedly vanquished the beast!"

The rest of the Guardians just looked at him...except Groot, who threw a rock at him because he was still mad about the stereo. Drax looked down at him, puzzled. "What?"

With the monster vanquished, the Guardians could get cleaned up and collect their payment from the Sovereign. Rocket was fiddling with one of the machines on the platform that hadn't been wrecked in the fight. "What are they called again?" Drax asked as he wiped the green goo from his face.

"Anulax batteries," Rocket said.

"Arbulary batteries," Drax said.

Star-Lord looked over. "That's nothing like what he just said. Those things are worth thousands of units apiece, which is why the Sovereign hired us to protect them. Careful what you say around these folks. They're easily offended, and the cost of transgression is death."

The team walked to the edge of the platform to meet the high priestess Ayesha, ruler of the Sovereign.

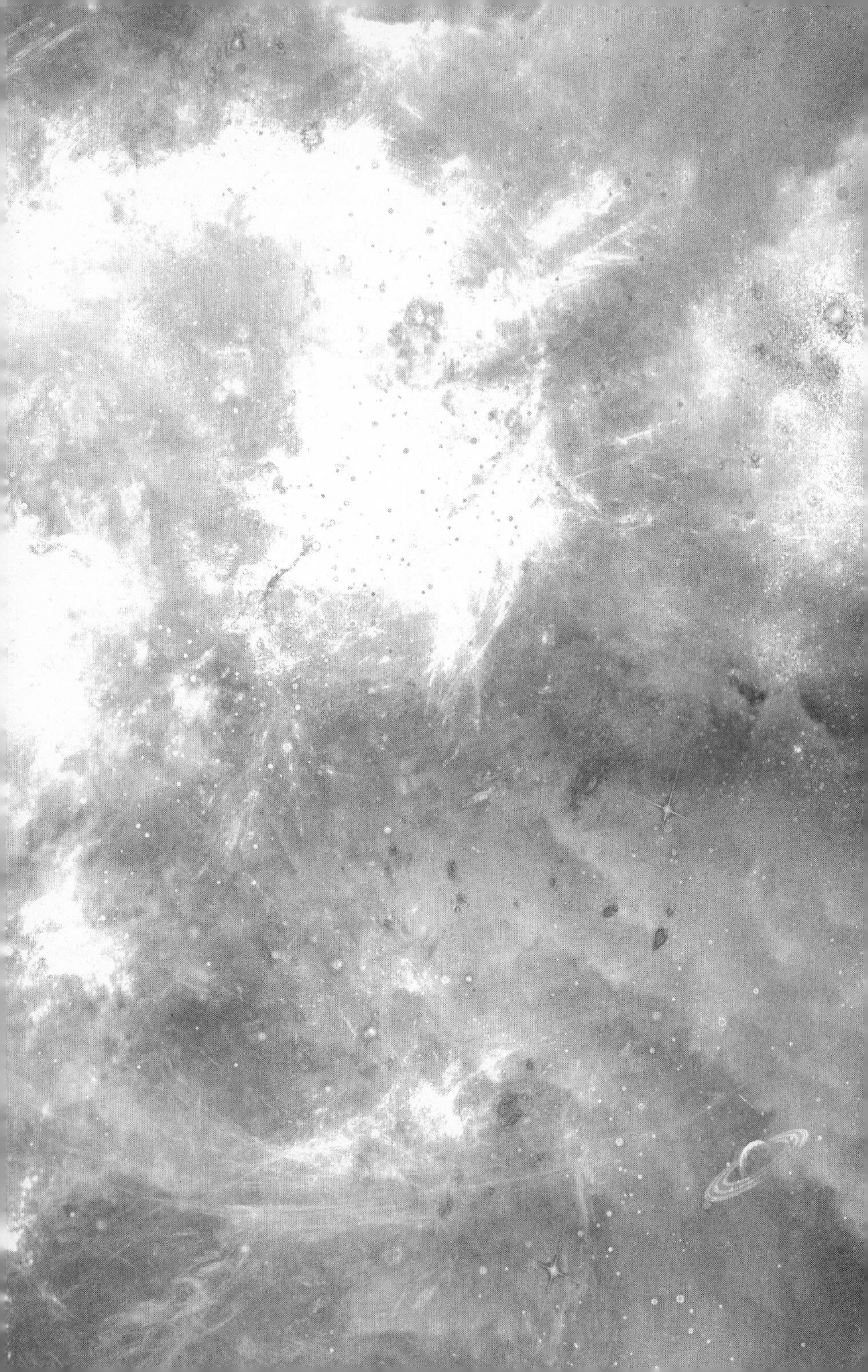

CHAPTER 2

We thank you, Guardians, for putting your lives on the line," Ayesha said from her throne in the great hall. The Guardians stood in a half circle before her. She was flanked by golden-robed Sovereign. Everything was gold: the throne, their hosts' skin and hair, the decorations in the hall. Only the walls and floor were different, decorated in a blue-and-black starburst design. "We could not risk the lives of our own Sovereign citizens. Every citizen is born exactly as designed by the community. Impeccable, both physically and mentally.

We control the DNA of our progeny, germinating them in birthing pods."

"Please," Gamora said. She stepped forward. "Your people promised something in exchange for our services. Bring it, and we shall gladly be on our way."

Ayesha lifted a finger and two Sovereign soldiers appeared from the side of the throne, dragging a figure with a hood over its head. Pushing the figure to its knees, the guards removed the hood.

Nebula. She simply glared at her sister, Gamora, who gazed steadily back.

"Family reunion, yay," Peter said, trying to lighten the mood a little. There was serious bad blood between the sisters. Nebula had remained loyal to their father, Thanos, and tried to kill Gamora and the rest of the Guardians the last time they had saved the galaxy. That adventure had ended with Peter holding one of the Infinity Stones in his hand, and defeating Ronan, a Kree fanatic, face-to-face. Nobody knew where Thanos was at the moment, but now at least the Guardians had Nebula under their control.

"I understand this is your sister," Ayesha said.

"She's worth no more to me than the bounty due for

her on Xandar," Gamora said. She hauled Nebula to her feet.

Ayesha stood. "Our soldiers apprehended her trying to steal the batteries. Do with her as you please."

Gamora pulled Nebula toward the door at the rear of the hall. Peter gave a slight bow. "We thank you, High Priestess Ayesha." He turned to go, but she had one last question.

"What is your heritage, Mr. Quill?"

Peter stopped, surprised by the question. "My mother is from Earth."

"And your father?"

"He ain't from Missouri," Peter quipped. "That's all I know."

"I see within you an unorthodox genealogy," Ayesha said. "A hybrid that seems…particularly reckless."

Peter didn't know who his father was. His mother had always claimed he was a spaceman, but Peter had written that off to confusion caused by the brain cancer that eventually overtook her. Now Ayesha had brought up all that old sadness, and Peter didn't know what to say. He did know he was pretty mad.

"You know," Rocket piped up, "they told me you

people were conceited, but that isn't true at all." He shot Peter an obvious wink. The assembled Sovereign nobles gasped at the insult. Soldiers raised their weapons. "Ah, I'm using my wrong eye again, aren't I?" Rocket said when he noticed that they'd seen through his sarcasm. "I'm sorry; that was meant to be behind your back."

Peter turned and walked out of the throne room before things could get any tenser. Drax picked up Rocket and followed. "Count yourself blessed they don't kill you," Drax whispered when he put Rocket back down outside the throne room.

Rocket grinned up at him and lifted the flap on his shoulder bag. It was stuffed with Anulax batteries. "You're telling me. Wanna buy some batteries?"

He and Drax laughed the rest of the way back to the ship.

CHAPTER 3

The Guardians wasted no time getting away from the Sovereign. Rocket powered up the *Milano*. "All right, let's get Baldy to Xandar and collect that bounty!" he said. The *Milano* streaked across the sky over the magnificent capital city, then up into space. Groot, plastered to the rear window, watched wide-eyed as the planet receded behind them.

Peter left the piloting to Rocket. He needed a change of clothes after the fight. He put on some music from

Awesome Mix Vol. 2 and looked around for a clean shirt. It wasn't easy to do laundry in space.

Nearby, Gamora was putting a new pair of shackles on Nebula's wrists. Nebula glared but did not try to resist.

"That stuff about my father," Peter said, sulking and angry. "Who does she think she is?"

"I know you're sensitive about that," Gamora said with a little chill in her voice.

"I'm not sensitive about it. I just don't know who he is." He could tell from the look she gave him that something else was on her mind, and Peter thought he knew what it was. "Sorry if it seemed like I was flirting with the high priestess. I wasn't."

"I don't care if you were," she said, leading Nebula away toward the front of the ship.

"I feel like you do care," he called after her. "That's why I'm apologizing. So, sorry."

"Gamora's not the one for you, Quill," Drax said from behind him. Peter jumped. He hadn't noticed Drax standing back there in the shadows.

"There are two types of beings in the universe," Drax said. "Those who dance and those who do not."

Peter nodded, humoring him. He wasn't about to take romantic advice from Drax. "I first met my beloved at a war rally. Everyone in the village flailed about, dancing, except one woman: my Ovette. I knew immediately she was the one for me. The most melodic song in the world could be playing and she wouldn't even tap her foot. Wouldn't move a muscle. One might assume she was dead."

"I get it. I'm a dancer; Gamora is not," Peter said.

"You just need to find a woman who is pathetic. Like you." Somehow, Peter didn't feel any better.

Gamora started locking Nebula to a beam toward the rear of the *Milano*'s passenger compartment. Nearby was a bowl of fruit. Nebula reached for it but Gamora jerked her arm back and locked her in place with the bowl just out of reach. "I'm hungry," Nebula said.

"No," Gamora said. "It's not ripe yet."

Nebula didn't believe her. "I hate you," she said.

"You hate me," Gamora echoed, starting to return to the bridge.

"You left me there while you stole that stone for yourself," Nebula said. "And yet here you stand, a hero. I will be free of these shackles soon enough and I will kill you. I swear." Hate shone in her black eyes even though she never raised her voice.

Gamora turned back to her. "No. You're going to live out the rest of your days in a prison on Xandar, wishing you could."

Suddenly, alarms sounded throughout the ship. Gamora left Nebula to head for the cockpit and see what was happening.

"This is weird," Peter said. "We've got a Sovereign fleet approaching from the rear."

Rocket was in the other pilot's seat. Drax stood behind them. "Why would they do that?" Gamora asked as she got settled in the navigator's seat behind Peter and Rocket.

"Probably because Rocket stole some of the batteries," Drax said.

Rocket spun in his seat. "Dude!"

"Right," Drax said more quietly. "He didn't steal some of those. I don't know why they're out there. What a mystery this is." His expression barely changed—Drax was a terrible liar.

The Sovereign ships opened fire all at once. Blasts of energy rocked the *Milano* and streaked through space on all sides. Peter threw the ship into a series of twisting evasive maneuvers, speeding away toward a jump point. There had to be one nearby.

"What were you thinking?!" Peter shouted over the impacts.

"Dude, they were really easy to steal!"

"That's your defense?" Gamora was incredulous.

"Come on, you saw how that high priestess talked down to us. Now I'm teaching her a lesson."

"Oh, I didn't realize your motivation was altruism," Peter said. "It's really a shame the Sovereign have mistaken your intentions and are trying to kill us."

"Exactly!"

"I was being sarcastic!"

"Oh no, you're supposed to use your sarcastic voice! Now I look foolish!"

"Can we put the bickering on hold until we survive this massive space battle?" Gamora snapped.

"More incoming," Peter warned.

"Good," Rocket snarled. "I'm gonna kill some guys." He roared and blazed away at the Sovereign ships, destroying several of them. The rest dipped and swerved, coming around for another pass at the *Milano*.

"You're not killing anyone," Gamora said. "All those ships are remotely piloted."

Ayesha watched everything unfold from a balcony overlooking a huge space full of simulator rigs. Dozens of Sovereign were piloting the drones, shouting in frustration when their craft were destroyed.

"Admiral," Ayesha said to the official standing next to her. "What is the delay?"

"High Priestess—the batteries," the admiral said carefully. "They are exceptionally combustible and could destroy our entire fleet." The admiral had told his pilots to use extreme caution for this reason. They might not be manned, but the Soverign Fleet was still extremely valuable.

"Our concern is their slight against our people. We

hire them and they steal from us?" Ayesha hissed. "This is heresy of the highest order."

The admiral nodded and spoke into a microphone linked to every remote pilot. "All command modules. Fire with the intent to kill."

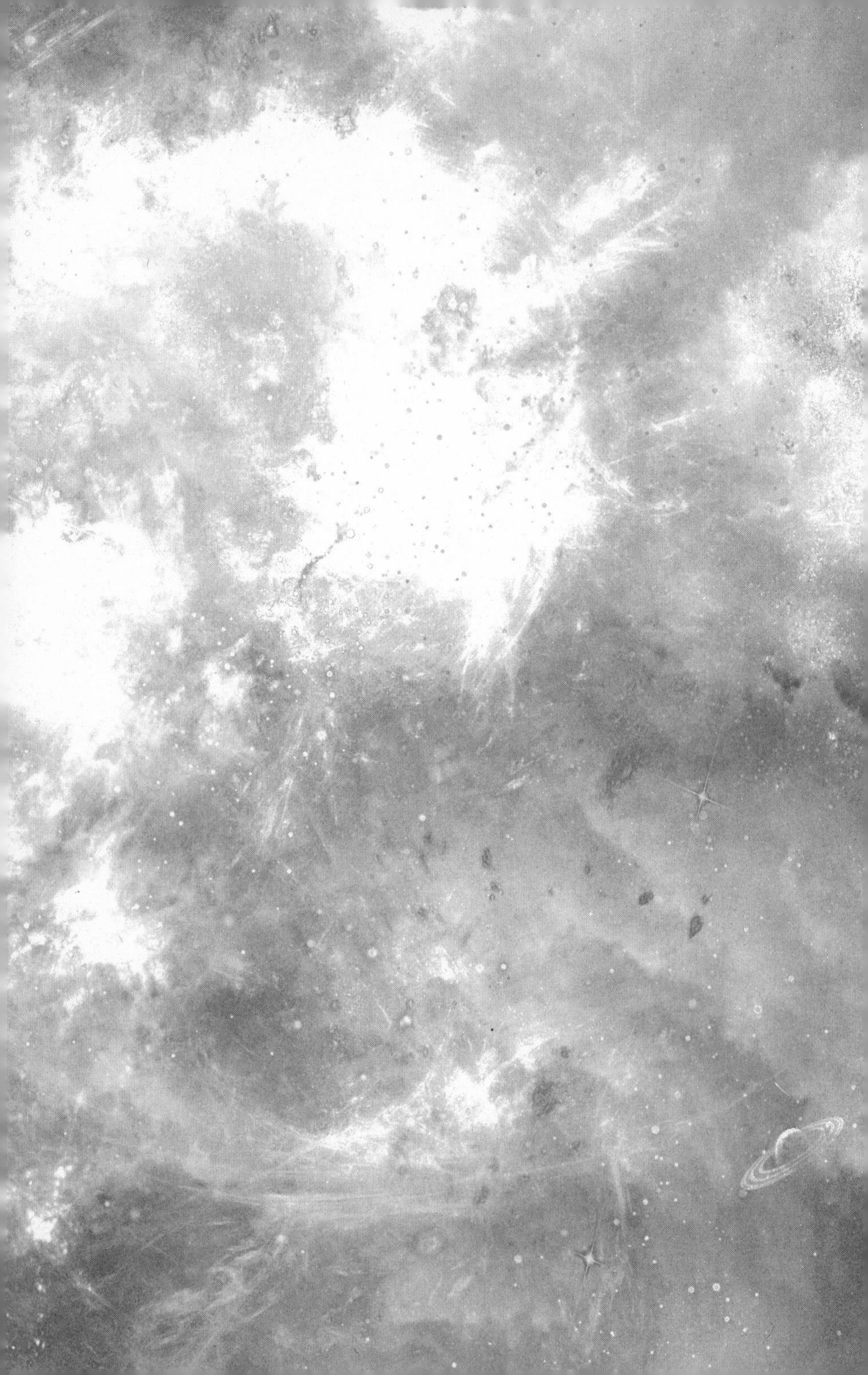

CHAPTER 4

What's the closest habitable planet?" Peter called out.
Gamora consulted the star chart. "It's called Berhert."

"How many jumps?"

"Only one, but the access point is forty-seven klicks away...and you have to go through that quantum asteroid field." Peter looked ahead and saw the flashes of colliding asteroids. A quantum asteroid field was like a regular asteroid field, except the asteroids flashed randomly in and out of existence. It was some kind of anomaly in the fabric of space-time. Peter wasn't sure how it worked, but it was no easy thing to survive flying through a place where an asteroid might appear randomly right in front of you at any moment.

"Quill. To make it through that, you would have to be the greatest pilot in the universe," Drax said.

"Lucky for us..." Peter began.

"I am," Rocket said before Peter could finish his sentence. Rocket switched the *Milano* to his controls and put it into a spiraling dive through the outer edges of the field. An asteroid appeared just ahead and he barely dodged it. Behind them, the Sovereign drones followed. Asteroids smashed many of them to flaming bits, but the rest kept coming.

Annoyed, Peter stabbed the console and took back control of the ship. Rocket slammed his steering column back and forth. "What are you doing?"

"I've been flying this ship since I was ten years old."

"I was cybernetically engineered to fly a spacecraft!"

They wrestled over the controls, switching them back and forth as the *Milano* jerked crazily, missing asteroids by sheer luck. "Stop it," Gamora said.

"Later on tonight," Rocket said, "you're going to be

lying down in your bed and there's going to be something squishy in your pillowcase, and you're going to go, 'What's this?' and it's gonna be because I put a turd in there."

"You put your turd in my bed, I shave you," Peter threatened. He took control again.

"Oh, it won't be my turd," Rocket shot back. "It'll be Drax's."

Drax burst out laughing. "I have famously huge turds."

Gamora looked at the three of them, one after another, disbelief plain on her face. "We're about to die and this is what we're discussing?"

Rocket took back control.

"Dude, seriously," Peter said, and they both stabbed at their control buttons. While they were fighting, an asteroid appeared close enough to crash into the rear of the *Milano*, sending the ship into an uncontrolled spin. Pieces of its hull broke away, exposing the passenger compartment to the vacuum of space. Nebula was nearly sucked out into the void. The only things holding her were the shackles. She kicked and screamed, though nobody could hear her.

Up in the cockpit, Groot went flying toward the back. Peter reached out and caught him, then tossed him to Drax. Then he touched a series of screens that activated emergency shielding. The hull breach sealed and Nebula crashed back to the floor.

"Idiots!" she screamed.

"Well," Rocket said, "that's what you get when Quill flies."

Gamora threw a loose piece of junk at him, hitting him in the back of the head. "We still have a Sovereign craft behind us." She read the navigator's heads-up display as the *Milano* dodged the fire from the last Sovereign drone.

"Our weapons are down," Peter said.

Gamora got a read on the jump portal. "Twenty klicks to the jump!" Drax handed Groot to her and she looked down at him. "Hold on," she told him.

They were most of the way through the quantum asteroid field. The jump portal glowed ahead, like a hole in space-time filled with multicolored energy. But they couldn't shake the last drone.

Drax went to the rear. He had an idea. Nebula was at full stretch on the floor, reaching for a piece of the fruit that had spilled out of the basket. Drax kicked it away. "It's not ripe."

He hooked a heavy cable to his belt and stood in front of the rear airlock. Set into the wall was a rack of small discs. Below them a sign said SPACESUITS IN CASE OF EMERGENCY. Below that, someone had made a hand-written addition: OR FOR FUN.

Drax slapped one of the discs on his back and a force field surrounded his body. It would protect him against the vacuum and supply him with air for as long as he needed.

He stepped into the airlock and punched the button to open the outside hatch.

On Sovereign, the pilots of the destroyed drones gathered around the last remaining pilot as he leaned into his simulator. "Come on, Zylak, you can do this," one of them encouraged.

Zylak stayed tight to the fleeing ship, firing nonstop. The Sovereign pilot was good and Zylak scored a few direct hits. But he was getting the range, and the ship had no rear-mounted guns, so he didn't have to worry about incoming fire.

Then he saw something incredible. One of the Guardians jumped out of the ship's airlock attached to a cable. He jerked to a violent stop as the cable reached its full length. It was the bald, muscular Guardian, his body surrounded by the glimmer of a space suit…and he had a heavy gun in his hands. He raised the gun.

"Die, spaceship!" Drax roared into space. He got a bead on the drone and blew it away with a single shot.

In the Sovereign pilots' chamber, there was a brief silence. Zylak stared into the empty simulator.

CHAPTER 5

Approaching jump point," Gamora said. Peter locked in the coordinates and gunned the *Milano* forward... and a new swarm of Sovereign drones appeared.

"Son of a...they went around the field!" exclaimed Peter.

The drones raked the *Milano* with their combined fire, rocking the ship as it tried to cover the last distance to the portal. Peter wasn't sure they were going to make it in one piece.

Then, in a single instant, the entire Sovereign fleet

disappeared in a huge cluster of fireballs. When the afterimage cleared, a single spacecraft hung by itself in the void.

Shock silenced the Sovereign pilots' chamber. They had been sure their ambush would work. "Someone destroyed all our ships!" the admiral exclaimed.

Ayesha pierced him with an ice-cold glare. "Who?"

"One klick!" Gamora yelled. Sparks showered from overloaded circuits in the cockpit.

Rocket looked out the window at the ship that had just annihilated the Sovereign drones. "What is that?" he wondered. It didn't look like any ship he'd ever seen before.

"Who cares?" Peter was focused on one thing and one thing only. "That's the jump point!"

"It's a guy," Rocket said, amazed. An egg-shaped spacecraft, gleaming silvery white, flashed by them. A single humanoid form stood on top of it, holding a pair of glimmering cables as if they were the reins of a horse-drawn chariot. The figure raised a hand and waved.

Peter didn't care. He aimed the *Milano* at the jump portal and shot through it. The shock of the jump overloaded parts of the hull and the ship started spewing fire as it passed into Berhert's upper atmosphere. Pieces of it tumbled away, and the temporary shielding failed. Wind tore through the passenger compartment, sucking out debris and spewing it directly at Drax, still dangling at the end of his cable.

"Oh my God," Gamora said. "He's still out there."

She dashed back to the rear and caught the cable's spool just before it broke free of the wall. Nebula flailed in the wind, held in place by her manacles. The suction dragged Gamora out of the ship, but she caught hold of the edge of the hole and held on for dear life, the cable fixture in her other hand—and Drax still bouncing at the end of the cable. The friction of reentry started to burn around them, and soon they were trailing fire just like the rest of the ship.

Only then did Peter notice that both Drax and Gamora were outside the ship. He looked over his shoulder and saw Groot sitting in Drax's seat, calmly having a snack. "Groot, put your seat belt on. Prepare for a really bad landing!"

Peter kept the landing angle as shallow as he could, but they were going in fast and headed for a dense forest. The *Milano* tore through the canopy and then snapped off tree trunks for a mile or more before plowing into the ground and coming to rest in a cloud of dust. A final shower of shattered branches and drifting leaves fell around the crash site, and with a groan, the *Milano*'s right wing broke off and crashed to the ground. A startled flock of birds flew up into the sky.

Behind the ship, Drax pushed himself up and started laughing. "That was awesome! Yes!"

Gamora stood closer to the ship, still holding the other end of Drax's cable. She flung it to the ground. "Look at this!" she screamed as Peter and Rocket emerged from the wreck. They brought Nebula out, too, not wanting her to be trapped inside the ship if it collapsed any further. She might have been a prisoner, but she was still Gamora's sister.

"Where's the other half of our ship?! Either one of you could have gotten us through that field!" Gamora said. "Peter," she snapped, "we almost died because of your arrogance."

"No, because he stole the Anulax batteries!" Peter pointed at Rocket.

"They're called Harbulary batteries," Drax said.

"No, they're not!" Peter yelled.

"You know why I did it, Star-Munch?" Rocket said.

Offended, Peter looked away. "I'm not gonna answer to 'Star-Munch.'"

"I did it because I wanted to! What are we even talking about this for? We just had a little man save us by blowing up fifty ships!"

"How little?" Drax asked.

"I don't know," Rocket said. He held up his left hand with thumb and forefinger maybe an inch apart. "Like…this?"

Gamora was obviously skeptical. "A little one-inch man saved us?"

"Well, if he got closer, I'm sure he'd be much larger."

"Yeah, that's how eyesight works, you stupid raccoon," Peter said.

"Don't call me a raccoon!" Rocket yelled, furious. Peter *knew* he hated that word.

"I'm sorry," Peter said seriously. "I took it too far. I meant 'trash panda.'"

Rocket looked around, confused. "Is that better?"

"I don't know," Drax said.

Peter couldn't help himself. He started to laugh. "It's worse. It's so much worse."

"You son of a—" Rocket launched himself at Peter, but before they could really fight, all the Guardians looked up, hearing the thrum of a spaceship's engine.

"Someone followed you through the jump point," Nebula said. "Set me free. You'll need my help."

"You're a fool, Nebula," Gamora scoffed.

"You're a fool to deprive yourself of my talent in combat."

"You'd attack me the moment I let you go."

"No, I won't," Nebula said quickly, looking around at the group and trying to appear earnest.

"You'd think an evil supervillain would be better at lying," Peter commented.

The ship came into view, the same pale, egg-shaped craft Rocket had seen near the jump point on the edge of the quantum asteroid field. The Guardians clustered together, ready to fight if they had to. Groot was behind them, just then climbing down out of the ship. "I bet it's the one-inch man," Drax said.

Yellow lights blazed powerfully from the craft's windows as it settled among the trees near where the *Milano* had crashed. After it came to rest, two figures appeared from a large, eye-shaped portal in its side. One was a slim humanoid alien in green and black, with large black eyes and a pair of small antennae pointing up from her forehead. The other was a human male in a long cloak, his bearded face alight with a smile as he looked the Guardians over. "After all these years, I've found you," he said to Peter.

"And who *are* you?" Peter shot back.

"I figured my rugged good looks would make that obvious," the man said. "My name is Ego...and I'm your dad, Peter."

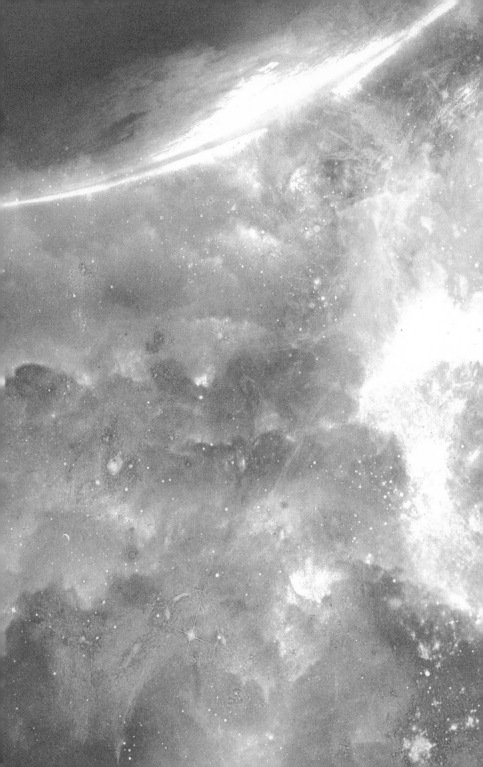

CHAPTER 6

The world of Contraxia was one of the galaxy's most notorious places for bad behavior, and Yondu Udonta felt right at home there…at least, usually. But right then he was uneasy, because Contraxia was a well-known Ravager hangout, and Yondu was in more than a little trouble with the Ravagers. He had done some work that, to the other Ravagers, looked like kidnapping—which was a serious violation of the Ravager code. They might have been pirates and killers, but they had rules.

It was up to Yondu to explain himself, and he'd

been brooding over how to do it since some of his fellow Ravagers had let him know that Stakar Ogord, the top chief of the Ravagers, was visiting Contraxia. Now some of Yondu's shipmates were calling to him, letting him know that Stakar was in this same part of town. He got himself ready and came down the stairs into the open hall. Flanked by two loyal Ravagers, Wretch and Halfnut, he worked his way through the crowd to see Stakar with one of his top lieutenants, Martinex. "Stakar," he said, and thumped a fist against his chest twice in the Ravager salute. "It's been some time."

"Seems like this establishment is the wrong kind of disreputable," Stakar sneered after a long, disdainful look at Yondu. He turned and walked away.

"Stakar!" Yondu called after him. He'd known he would be in trouble after word got around about him and Peter Quill, but this was worse than he'd expected.

"There are a hundred factions of Ravagers," Stakar said to the owner of the bar. "You just lost the business of ninety-nine by serving one."

"Sir, please," the owner begged, but Stakar shoved her away.

Yondu's shock turned to anger. He shattered his glass

and strode forward, screaming, "I don't care what you think of me!"

Stakar spun and stalked back toward him. "So what are you following us for?"

"You're gonna listen to what I've got to say!"

"I don't gotta listen to nothing! You betrayed the code! Ravagers don't deal in kids!"

"I told you before: I didn't know what was going on!"

"You didn't know because you didn't want to know. Because it made you rich."

"I demand a seat at the table!" Yondu showed Stakar the Ravager patch on his coat. "I wear these flames just like you."

"You may dress like one of us, but you'll never hear the Horns of Freedom when you die, Yondu. And the colors of Ogord will never flash over your grave." Stakar grabbed Yondu's lapels and spoke more quietly. "If you think I take pleasure in exiling you, you're wrong. You broke all our hearts."

With that, Stakar walked away. Martinex lingered a moment longer, then followed. Yondu stood alone, shocked by the words of exile.

"Pathetic," growled one of the other Ravagers who

was watching the scene with his compatriots. "First, Quill betrays us and Yondu just lets him go scot-free. We followed him because he was the one who wasn't afraid to do what needed to be done. It seems he's gone soft."

"If he's so soft," said Kraglin, another Ravager, "why are you whispering for?"

"You know I'm right, Kraglin."

A third Ravager by the name of Tullk piped up. "You best be careful when you say that about our captain." He started to go on, but there was a stir from the crowd nearby and all the Ravagers turned to see what was going on.

It was a small party of gold-skinned Sovereign nobles, with their high priestess Ayesha in the center, stepping carefully on a blue carpet two attendants rolled out in front of her so she wouldn't have to touch the ground of an unworthy place like Contraxia. She stopped at the end of the rug, directly in front of Yondu.

"Yondu Udonta," she said. "I have a proposition for you."

CHAPTER 7

Peter couldn't believe that after all these years, his father had just shown up out of the blue and saved all their lives from the Sovereign. But Ego—what a name—knew things about Peter that only his father could know, and part of Peter wanted Ego's story to be true. After all these years, maybe he could start to know his father. It seemed too good to be true.

They all sat around a campfire near the wreck of the *Milano*, as Ego caught Peter up on all that had happened while they were separated. "I hired Yondu to pick you up after your mother passed away," Ego was saying. "But instead of returning you, Yondu kept you. I have no clue as to why."

"I'll tell you why," Peter said. "I was a skinny little kid who could squeeze into places adults couldn't. Made it easier for thieving."

Ego considered this. "Well, I've been trying to track you down ever since."

"I thought Yondu was your father," Drax said. He was sitting just out of the firelight, eating and listening in on the conversation.

Peter couldn't believe it. "What? We've been together this whole time and you thought Yondu was my actual blood relative?"

"You look exactly alike," Drax explained with his mouth full.

"One's blue!" Rocket said incredulously.

"No, he's not my father," Peter said. "Yondu is the guy who abducted me, kicked the snot out of me to teach me to fight, and kept me in terror by threatening to eat me."

"Eat you?" Ego repeated.

"Yeah."

"Ah…" Ego said, angrily realizing just how Peter must have grown up.

"How did you locate us now?" Gamora asked. She had been quiet so far. Peter had a feeling she didn't quite trust what was happening…and neither did Peter, as much as he wanted to. They would have to talk about it.

"Well, even where I reside, out past the edge of what's known, we've heard tell of the man they call Star-Lord," Ego said. He stood and gestured toward his ship. "What say we head out there right now?" he asked Peter. "Your associates are welcome, even that triangle-faced monkey there." Rocket touched his muzzle with both hands. "I promise you," Ego went on, "it's unlike any other place you've ever seen. And there, I can explain your very special heritage. Finally get to be the father I've always wanted to be. Excuse me. Gotta take a whiz."

When he was gone, Peter looked across the campfire at Gamora. "I'm not buying it," he said quietly.

"Let's go take a walk," she suggested.

"I am Mantis," Ego's companion said, introducing herself to Drax after Peter and Gamora had gone. Her face split in a grimace and she stared at him.

"What are you doing?" he asked.

"Smiling. I hear it is the thing to do to make people like you."

"Not if you do it like that."

"Oh. I was raised alone on Ego's planet. I do not understand the intricacies of social interaction." She looked over at Rocket, who was grooming himself at the edge of the fire. "Can I pet your puppy? He's adorable."

Drax looked from her to Rocket and back, his expression as neutral as he could make it. "Yes," he said.

She reached out and stroked the back of Rocket's head. He snarled and snapped at her, and she jumped back with a little scream. Drax laughed loud and long. "That is called a practical joke!"

Mantis started to laugh, too. "I like it very much."

"I just made it up!" Drax was still laughing. On the far side of the campfire, Nebula sat alone, watching them.

"Give me a break," Peter said when he and Gamora were a little distance away from the campfire. "After all this time, you show up, and you're just going to be my dad? This could be a trap. The Kree purists, the Ravagers—they all want us dead."

"I know, but..." Gamora looked troubled.

"But what?"

"What was that story you told me about Zardu Hasselfrau?"

"Who?" Peter had absolutely no idea who or what she was talking about.

"He owned a magic boat."

Ah, Peter thought, remembering the story he had told Gamora ages ago. "Right. Not a magic boat, a talking car," he said.

"Why did it talk again?"

"To help him fight crime, and to be supportive."

"As a child, you would carry his picture in your pocket and you would tell all the other children that he was your father but he was out of town," Gamora said, recalling what he'd told her once.

"Touring with his band in Germany," Peter said, finishing the story. "Why are you bringing it up now?"

"I love that story," she said.

Peter was surprised to hear she felt that way. "I hate that story," he said. "It's so sad. As a kid I used to see all the other kids off playing catch with their dads, and I wanted that more than anything in the world."

"That's my point, Peter. Listen." She stepped close to him and took his hands softly. "If he ends up being evil, we'll just kill him."

Peter looked down at her hands holding his. She stepped back and let him go.

But she's right, he thought. What if this really was his father? Could he stand to not find out?

By morning, the decision was made. Peter, Drax, and Gamora were going to Ego's planet to learn about Peter's origins. The others would stay and repair the *Milano*. Rocket and Groot didn't like the plan, and neither did Nebula. "You're leaving me with that fox?!" she raged when she found out.

"He's not a fox," Gamora said. She looked at Rocket. "Shoot her if she does anything suspicious."

"Uh-huh," Rocket said. He was busy with a matter compiler, using it to rebuild the damaged parts of the ship's interior.

"Or if you feel like it," Gamora added.

"Good." Rocket was ignoring her, feeling a little selfish and angry that the Guardians were splitting up.

Groot sat sadly nearby. He knew some of them were leaving but didn't understand why. "It'll just be a couple of days," Gamora explained to him. "We'll be back before Rocket's finished fixing the ship."

Groot waved as she walked away to join Peter and Drax, who were waiting with all the gear they were taking on the trip to Ego's home planet. "What if the Sovereign come?" Drax was asking Peter.

"There's no way for them to know we're here," Peter said. He was irritated that everyone saw all kinds of problems with the plan, when to him it was the obvious thing to do. "You're like an old woman."

"Because I am wise?" Drax countered.

Peter didn't know what to say to that, so he ignored it. Before they left, he stopped to say something to Rocket, but Rocket was in no mood to hear it. "Hope Daddy isn't as big a jerk as you, orphan boy."

So much for talking things out, Peter thought. Maybe Rocket was still mad about their fight in the asteroid field, or maybe he just thought Peter was stupid to trust Ego. Either way, Peter was sick of it. "What is your goal here?" he asked. "To get everybody to hate you? Because it's working." Rocket didn't answer. After a moment, Peter walked toward Ego's ship, flanked by Drax and Gamora.

A moment later the ship lifted away. Nebula watched. She knew her chance would come if she was patient.

CHAPTER 8

Aboard Ego's ship, everything was rounded and smooth and white. The three Guardians had barely settled in when Ego excused himself to lie down in a recessed couch in a small room off the main space. Mantis went with him. After he lay down, she touched his forehead and whispered, "Sleep."

Ego's eyes closed.

Peter watched from across the room. When Ego was asleep, Peter lingered there for a long time. His conversation with Gamora was fresh in his mind. He took his wallet out of his pocket, the same wallet he'd carried when he was ten years old. Inside was a worn picture of the man he had pretended was his father. Peter looked at it for a long time. After so many years, could this really be happening? And was it really connected to his ability to hold an Infinity Stone in his hand back on Xandar?

Another question rang in his mind: *Who am I, really?*

Only Ego could answer.

After a while, he found Drax and Mantis sitting together. Peter joined them around a couch that was round and white like everything else. "Hey," Peter said to Mantis. "Can I ask you a personal question?"

"No one has ever asked me a personal question," she said, which he took to be permission.

"Your antennae. What are they for?"

"Their purpose?"

"Yes," Drax interrupted. "Quill and I have a bet."

Peter dropped his head in disappointment. "You're not supposed to say that."

Drax ignored him. "I say that if you are about to go through a doorway and it is too low, they save you from being decapitated."

"Right," Peter said. "And if it's anything other than you *specifically* being decapitated by a doorway, I win."

"They are not for feeling doorways," Mantis said, taking the question seriously. "I think they have something to do with my empathic abilities."

Gamora had entered through the closest doorway. "What are those?"

"When I touch someone, I can feel their feelings," Mantis explained.

"You mean read minds?"

"No. Telepaths read thoughts. Empaths feel feelings. Emotions." She turned to Peter. "May I?"

"Oh, all right," Peter said. He was curious.

She put a hand on his and her antennae glowed a bright white. "You feel...love," she said.

Immediately, Peter was uncomfortable. "Yeah, I guess, I feel a general unselfish love for everybody—"

"No," she said. "Romantic love."

Uh-oh, Peter thought. He knew where this was going. "No, no I don't—"

Delighted, Mantis pointed at Gamora. "For her!"

"No, that's not—"

Drax roared with laughter, drowning out whatever

Peter had been about to say. "She just told everyone your deepest, darkest secret! You must be so embarrassed!" Still laughing, Drax turned to Mantis. He could barely contain his excitement; he slapped his chest. "Do me! Do me!"

Mantis leaned over and placed a hand on Drax's chest. A moment later she, too, burst out laughing. "I have never felt such humor!" she said, collapsing on the bench next to him.

She bounced up, still riding the wave of Drax's humor, and skipped over to Gamora—but when she reached to touch her, Gamora caught her gauntleted wrist and held it away. "Touch me, and the only thing you're going to feel is a broken jaw."

Mantis looked crestfallen. She turned back to Peter and Drax. "I can also alter emotions to some extent."

"Yeah, like what?" Peter asked.

"If I touch someone who is sad, I can ease them into contentment for a short while." She glanced over at Gamora. "I can use it to make a stubborn person compliant." Then she returned her attention to Peter. "But mostly I use it to help my master sleep. He lies awake at night, thinking about his progeny."

"Do one of those on me," Drax said.

Mantis walked over to him and laid a palm on his forehead. "Sleep," she said. Drax's head tipped back and he started snoring like a buzz saw.

That's a pretty good trick, Peter thought.

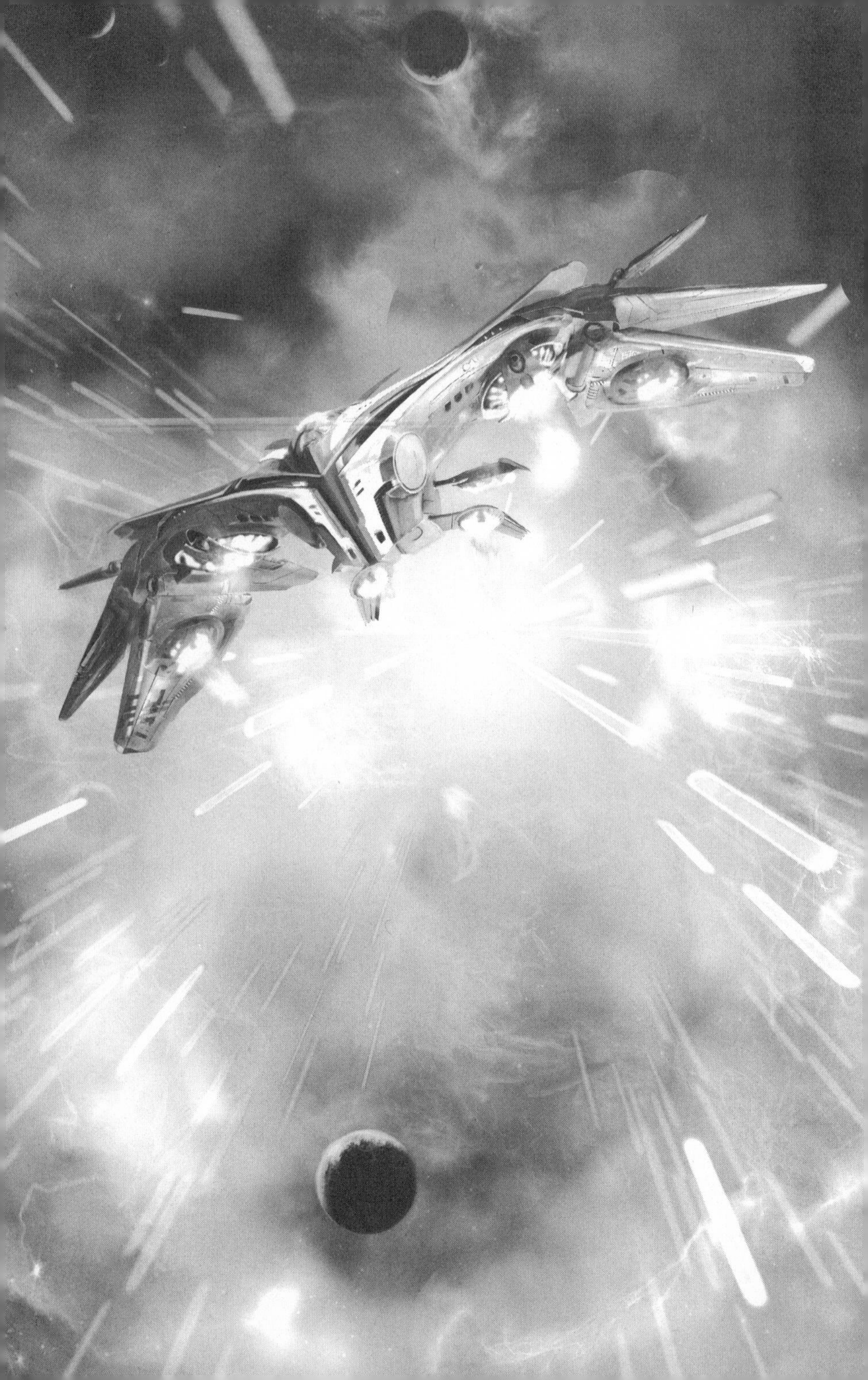

CHAPTER 9

Rocket heard the Ravager force approaching. He was out in the woods, watching the security precautions he had placed around the *Milano*, which he would need a few more days to repair. When he saw the Ravagers' flashlights in the trees, he figured he could just watch and wait, because the first group was headed right for a little present he'd left for any unwanted guests.

One of them stepped on a pressure plate hidden under some leaves. Dozens of tiny darts tipped with a powerful sedative shot out from the surrounding trees.

The Ravagers dropped to the ground without a sound, looking a bit like pincushions with all the darts stuck in them.

But more of them were coming, and as Rocket turned to scamper along a tree branch, one of them spotted him. They shot their blasters at him, shattering tree limbs and filling that part of the forest with smoke. He couldn't believe nobody at the *Milano* was hearing this...but it was just Groot and Nebula back there, anyway. No help coming from that direction.

He got to a safe spot, with the trunk of a huge, old tree between him and the Ravagers. They were standing right in the middle of a group of gravity field mines Rocket had strewn earlier that night. Now that they weren't shooting at him, Rocket triggered all the mines at once. Crackling blue energy flashed out from the mines, flinging the Ravagers into the air. Some of them bounced from one expanding energy field to another before crashing back to the ground. *Drax would have appreciated this*, Rocket thought. He laughed out loud as the last of that group of Ravagers hit the ground and lay still. Now it was time to take a little risk.

Rocket dropped out of the trees onto a Ravager. He

slapped a little relay circuit onto the Ravager's head. Then he jumped fast from Ravager to Ravager, planting a relay on each one and then jumping back up into the branches before they could get a fix on where he was. He touched a remote trigger and electricity jolted through every one of the relays. That whole part of the forest lit up with the flashes. When they faded, all the Ravagers were down.

Was that them all? Rocket dropped out of the trees. For a moment he thought he was alone, but then his nose did the work. He could smell Ravagers. Close by. Two of them.

"Ain't so tough now, are you? Without all your toys," one of them said. Rocket launched himself at the Ravager, scratching and biting at him. He heard the other Ravager raise his gun and jumped out of the way just as the blast of energy took down the first Ravager. His leap carried him back across the clearing to the second Ravager. Rocket pounded him to the ground and kept pounding him until he didn't try to get up anymore.

How many more could there be? He looked around and didn't see any.

But he did hear a whistle, and it was a whistle he recognized. Yondu. That meant—

Rocket glanced up to see the glowing red trail of Yondu's whistle-controlled arrow, shooting through the trees at him, way too fast to dodge. He reflexively ducked his head and the arrow stopped an inch short, aimed right between his eyes.

He looked up. "Crap."

"Hey there, rat," Yondu said with a grin, coming out of the trees with more Ravagers. A lot more.

"How's it going, you blue idiot?" Rocket answered.

"Not so bad. We got ourselves a pretty good little gig here. This golden gal with quite a high opinion of herself has offered us a large sum to deliver you and your pals over to her, because she wants to kill you."

The Ravagers laughed. Rocket stood there, the arrow still before him, wishing he'd never taken the stupid batteries in the first place. But they'd been right there…How was he supposed to resist something like that?

Inside the *Milano*, Nebula could hear part of what was going on. This was her chance…if she could convince Groot. "Your friend," she said. "There's too many of them. He needs my help."

Groot looked troubled.

"If you care about him, you need to get me out of these bonds," she said. "They're going to kill him."

Out in the clearing, Yondu kept his arrow hovering near Rocket. "I tell you, it was pretty easy to find you. I put a tracer on your ship back during the war with Ronan."

"Give me your word you won't hurt Groot and I'll tell you where the batteries are," Rocket said. He knew when he was beaten. He just had to try to make the best deal he could. Later he would be able to come up with an escape plan.

"Lucky for you my word don't mean squat," Yondu said. "Otherwise I'd actually hand you over."

Some of the Ravagers had started to laugh again, but now they stopped as they figured out what Yondu was saying. "Otherwise you what?" one of them said.

"We'll take those batteries," Yondu said. "They're worth what, a quarter of a million on the open market?"

"That priestess offered us a million," the other Ravager said. He was big and scarred and ugly and looked like he only lived for the next fight. "A quarter is only one-third of that!"

The other Ravagers started arguing about this. Rocket noticed none of them were very good at math. "Enough!" Yondu said. "The point is, we ain't stupid enough to kill the Guardians of the Galaxy! The whole dang Nova Corps would be on us!"

"That ain't right!" Kraglin called out. "I just gotta say this, Captain. No matter how many times Quill betrays us, you protect him. Like none of the rest of us much matter. I'm the one what sticks up for you!"

"Take it easy, Kraglin," another Ravager cautioned.

"He's gone soft," the ugly Ravager said. "Suppose it's time for a change in leadership!"

Weapons were raised. Voices got loud. Yondu's arrow lifted away from Rocket and hovered by Yondu's head, waiting for a target. "Whoa, whoa!" Rocket shouted over the tumult. "There must be some kind of peaceful resolution to this, fellas. Or even a violent one where I'm standing over *there*."

The Ravagers were still staring one another down. Would they mutiny against Yondu? Rocket started looking around for the quickest way out of the circle of knuckleheads with guns. He kept his eye on Yondu, figuring that if anything was going to start, it would start there—and it did, but not in the way he'd expected. Rocket was shocked to see the fin on Yondu's head, which he used to control the arrow, shatter in a burst of sparks. The blue-skinned Ravager looked stunned and woozy. He sank to his knees, revealing who had shot him.

Nebula.

Uh-oh, Rocket thought. One of the deadliest assassins in the galaxy was loose. How had she gotten out of the cuffs? Where was Groot?

He didn't have time to think it all through, because she shot him next, zapping him with a powerful stun charge. It knocked him flat on his back. "Well, hello, boys," Nebula said to the Ravagers. She coolly bit into a piece of fruit from the bowl Drax had kicked out of her reach, eager to taste what had been denied her this whole miserable time with the so-called Guardians of the Galaxy.

Then she grimaced and spit it out in disgust. "It's not ripe."

CHAPTER 10

From space, Ego's planet was red and glowing, with circular areas of bright blue where a powerful energy shone through from the interior…but when Ego's ship dropped through the atmosphere and neared the surface, it was a completely different story. Brilliant sunshine, perfect temperatures, the air full of wonderful smells… and everywhere Peter looked he saw lush forests, fascinating buildings, monumental art. He still wasn't sure this Ego person was on the level, but man, this planet would be worth exploring either way.

As the ship landed, a part of it separated into a hovering platform that flew smoothly toward a magnificent palace surrounded by statues. There was no sun nearby, but somehow a golden light suffused everything. "Welcome, everyone, to my world," Ego said proudly.

"Wow," Peter said. He felt like a kid again...maybe because he was around his father. "You have your own planet?"

"Well. No larger than your Earth's moon."

"Humility," Drax said. "I like it. I, too, am extraordinarily humble."

Rainbow bubbles floated nearby. Drax touched one with his finger and it broke apart into a cloud of smaller bubbles, each dancing with color. Drax laughed with delight.

Only Gamora seemed immune to the general mood. "You own a planet and can destroy two dozen spaceships without a suit. What are you, exactly?"

"I'm what's called a Celestial, sweetheart," Ego answered without missing a beat.

Peter had heard of the Celestials. Was this possible? If his father was a Celestial, what did that make *him*? "A Celestial...like a God?"

"Small *g*, son. At least on the days I'm feeling as humble as Drax." Ego chuckled and led the way into the palace, Mantis next to him and the three Guardians following behind.

The main hall of the palace was stupendous, with ceilings a hundred feet high supported by ornamented pillars. Light shone down through circular skylights twenty feet wide. Lining the hall on both sides were rows of oval fixtures three times the height of a human. The nearest one lit up with a holographic display: a glowing blue brain against a background of stars.

"I don't know where I came from, exactly," Ego said. "The first thing I remember is drifting in the cosmos...utterly and entirely alone. Over millions of years I learned to control the molecules around me. I grew smarter and stronger." In another oval, a new image appeared: a cross-section of Ego's planet, with the shining blue core of Ego's self at its center. "And I continued building from there, layer by layer, the very planet you walk on now. But I wanted more. I desired meaning. There must be some life out there in the universe besides just me, I thought, and so I set myself the task of finding it."

He walked to the next display, where a blue column rose from the center of the planet to the surface. Within it, a human form took shape: Ego, looking as he had in 1980 when Meredith Quill had fallen in love with him.

"I created what I imagined biological life to be like. Down to the most minute detail," Ego said, proud of his accomplishment.

"I've also got pain receptors and a digestive system and all the accompanying junk. I wanted to experience what it truly meant to be human as I set out amongst the stars. Until I found what I sought."

A new display showed Ego and a small pink alien. "Life!" he went on. "I was not alone in the universe after all."

Peter was fascinated by the story, but he wanted Ego to get to the point. "When did you meet my mother?"

Ego turned to face Peter. "Not long after," he said. The next display showed Ego and Meredith Quill. "It was with Meredith that I first experienced love. I called her my river lily." The oval fixture closed and opened again, like an eye. Ego and Meredith still stood together, but now she was pregnant. A blue glow shone from her belly. "And from that love, Peter...you."

Peter looked up at the image, overcome with emotion. After so long not knowing his origins, at last he was seeing them come to life, with his father telling the story he'd always yearned for.

"I've searched for you for so long," Ego said earnestly. "When I heard of a man from Earth who held an Infinity Stone in his hand without dying, I knew you must be the son of the woman I loved."

This was the moment when Peter's amazement collided with the sadness and anger he'd felt his whole life at not having a father. Looking Ego dead in the eye, he asked, "If you loved her, why did you leave her?"

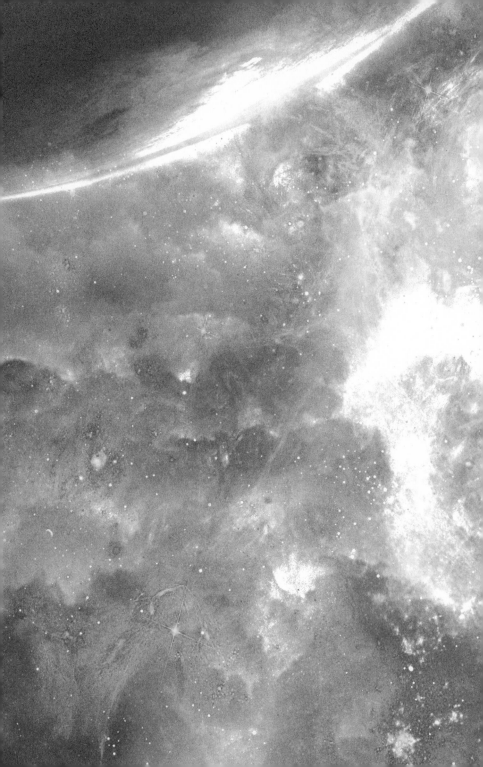

CHAPTER 11

On board the Ravager ship, things had gone from bad to worse almost as soon as they left Berhert. The talk of mutiny that had begun back on Contraxia exploded into violence. Yondu's own Ravagers betrayed him. They ambushed him and tied him to a chair before turning on the members of the crew who stayed loyal. Now they were dragging the loyalists one by one to the airlock and casting them out into space to die. As each one went out the airlock, a bloodthirsty cheer went up. Rocket was tied to another chair next to Yondu. In a cage hanging from the ceiling, Groot trembled in fear as the Ravagers shouted at him and taunted him.

All Yondu could do was watch.

"You're the one that killed those men," the ringleader of the mutiny said to him. "By leading them down the wrong path. Because you're weak!" He punched Yondu hard in the face. "And stupid!" Another punch. Yondu took them without making a sound. At least if he was getting punched in the face, his friends weren't going out the airlock.

The ringleader turned to the assembled Ravagers. "It's time for the Ravagers to once again rise to glory with a new captain—Taserface!"

The mutineers roared and cheered, but behind that was another sound.

Laughter.

Rocket sat in his chair, laughing so hard he strained against the ropes that bound him. When he saw Taserface glaring at him, he tried to stop. "I'm sorry. Your name...it's Taserface?"

"That's right," Taserface growled.

"You...shoot tasers out of your face?"

"It's metaphorical!" Taserface proclaimed. Another cheer went up.

"For what?" Rocket asked.

"For...It is a name what strikes fear into the hearts of anyone what hears it!" Taserface expected another cheer, but this time there were just murmurs among the Ravagers.

From the far end of the room, Nebula watched silently.

"Uh, okay," Rocket said, still trying not to laugh. "Whatever you say."

Taserface whipped out a knife. "You shut up. You're next." He turned back to Yondu. "Udonta. I have waited a long time—"

Rocket was laughing again. Taserface spun around and screamed, "What?!"

"I'm sorry. I am so sorry," Rocket said. "I just keep imagining you waking up in the morning, start looking in the mirror and in all seriousness saying to yourself"—he dropped his voice into a bad imitation of the Ravager—"'You know what would be a really cool name? Taserface!'" The Ravagers laughed, and so did

Rocket. "Hahaha, that's how I hear you in my head! What was your second choice?"

Taserface lunged forward and put the knife to Rocket's throat. "I'm killing you first."

"Well, dying is certainly better than having to live an entire life as a moron who thinks 'Taserface' is a cool name."

Taserface bared his teeth, but Nebula stepped out from the shadows. "That's enough killing for today."

"I thought you were the biggest sadist in the galaxy," Taserface said.

"That's when Daddy was paying the bills. The priestess wants to kill the fox herself." She nodded at Yondu. "And he has bounties on his head in at least twelve Kree provinces." Taserface moved to confront her, but she didn't look afraid. "I'm not as easy a mark as an old man without his magic stick or a talking woodland beast," she said. Taserface stopped. "I want ten percent of the take...and a couple more things."

Taserface glared, but he backed down. Nebula could have killed him, but she knew she'd made her point. A few minutes later, she went with Kraglin to see about updates to some of her cybernetic components that had been damaged when the Sovereign bounty hunters captured her. "We got a whole box of hands if that one don't work out," he said as she tried one.

"It's fine," she said, flexing the fingers.

"You, ah, think them Kree is gonna execute the cap'n?"

"The Kree consider themselves merciful," Nebula said. "It will be painless."

Kraglin took this in. "Well, uh, here it is," he said, showing her a docked fighter ship. That was the other thing she had demanded. "Best ship we got. Location of Ego's planet is in the nav. We'll wire you the ten percent once we's paid. What are you going to do with your share?"

She looked at the ship and spoke slowly, not looking at him. "As a child, my father would have Gamora and me battle one another in training. Every time my sister prevailed, my father would replace a piece of me with machinery, claiming he wanted me to be her equal. But she won. Again and again and again, never once refraining. So, after I murder my sister, I will buy a warship with every conceivable instrument of death. I will hunt my father like a dog and I will tear him apart, slowly, piece by piece, until he knows some sort of resemblance of the profound and unceasing pain I know every single day!"

"Yeah," Kraglin said uncertainly. "I was talking about, like, a pretty necklace or a nice hat. You know, something to make the other girls go, *'Oooh*, that's nice.'"

She didn't answer him. "Anyways," he said. "Happy trails." He clapped her on the shoulder and left. Five minutes later, Nebula was at the controls of the ship, heading for the nearest jump point.

CHAPTER 12

In a plaza outside the palace, Peter and Ego walked alone past a huge statue of Meredith Quill. They'd taken the conversation outside when it started to get personal.

"My mother told everyone my father was from the stars," Peter said, looking up at the statue. "She had brain cancer, so everyone thought she was delusional."

"Peter," Ego said, but Peter wasn't done. He had to get this off his chest.

"Listen," he said. "I'd love to believe all of this, I really would—but you left the most wonderful woman that ever was to die alone."

"I didn't want to leave your mother, Peter. If I don't return regularly to this planet and the light within it, this form will wither and perish."

"So why didn't you come back? Why did you send Yondu, a criminal of all people, to come and fetch me?"

"I loved your mother, Peter!" Ego's voice rose with emotion. "I couldn't stand to set foot on an Earth without her living! You can't imagine what that's like!"

"I know exactly what that feels like!" Peter shouted back. "I had to watch her die!"

Ego paused. When he spoke again, his voice was low and sad. "Over the millions and millions of years of my existence, I have made many mistakes, Peter, but you're not one of them. Please give me the chance to be the father she would want me to be. There's so much that I need to teach you about this planet and the light within. They are part of you, Peter."

"What do you mean?"

"Give me your hand, son." Ego took Peter's hands and brought them up level with his waist, as if he were

·about to catch something. "Here. Hold them like that."
Ego stepped back. "Now, close your eyes and concentrate. Take your brain to the center of this planet."

Peter did. He didn't know what Ego wanted, but...

Blue energy flashed in Peter's hands.

"Yes!" Ego shouted. "Yes!"

"Whoa!" Peter jumped and the light flashed out. "What was it?"

"Just relax," Ego said. "Concentrate. You can do it."

Peter tried again. The light came back and stayed this time, shimmering between his hands. "Yes. Now shape it," Ego said. "Feel that energy."

Slowly, eyes wide, Peter shaped the energy into a ball.

"Yes," Ego said. "You're home."

Peter grinned. Ego took a few more steps back and held out his hands. "Peter."

Peter tossed him the ball. Ego shaped it more and tossed it back—and just like that, Peter Quill was playing a game of catch with his father, just as he'd always wanted.

Near another door into the palace, Drax and Mantis sat on a broad golden staircase. "How'd you get to this weird, dumb planet?" he asked.

"Ego found me in my larval state. Orphaned on my home world. He took me in and raised me as his own," Mantis explained calmly.

"So you're a pet," he said.

She considered this. "I suppose so."

Drax enjoyed talking to her. She took everything he said at face value instead of getting offended at everything, like Quill. "People usually want cute pets. Why would Ego want such a hideous one?"

Shocked, she said, "I am hideous?"

"You are horrifying to look at, yes," Drax said. "But that's a good thing."

"Oh?"

"When you're ugly and someone loves you, you know they love you for who you are. Beautiful people never know who to trust."

"Well," Mantis said with a smile, "then I am certainly grateful to be ugly." They sat for a moment, looking out over the beauty of the planet without speaking.

Then Drax remembered something. "Those pools,"

he said, pointing to a courtyard at the bottom of the stairs. "They remind me of a time when I took my daughter to the forgotten lakes of my home world. She was like you."

"Disgusting?"

"Innocent," Drax said softly.

Mantis reached out and touched him gingerly on the shoulder. Her antennae glowed and she started to cry, feeling Drax's sadness at the memories of his family. "Drax?" she said when she stopped crying. "There's something I must tell you."

Gamora came through the door and Mantis stopped speaking. Gamora looked from her to Drax, sensing she'd walked in on something. "What's going on?"

Drax looked up at her. "This gross bug-lady is my new friend."

"I'm learning many things," Mantis said with a bright smile. "Like I'm a pet and ugly."

"You're not ugly," Gamora said.

Amazed, Drax said, "What are you talking about?"

Gamora ignored him. "Mantis, can you show us where we'll be staying?"

Mantis walked them to another part of the palace

complex. "Why are there no other beings on this planet?" Gamora asked.

"The planet is Ego," Mantis replied. "A dog would not invite a flea to live on his back."

"And you're not a flea?"

"I'm a flea with a purpose. I help him sleep."

Gamora waited a beat, then asked the question she'd wanted to get to all along. "What were you about to say to Drax before I walked out?"

Mantis looked uncomfortable. She glanced at Drax. "Nothing," she said. Then she started walking again. "Your quarters are this way."

CHAPTER 13

After Nebula left the Ravager ship, Taserface and the other mutinous Ravagers threw Rocket and Yondu into a cell. "We deliver you to the Kree in the morning," Taserface gloated. "Neither one of you will last much longer after that."

"Okay, Taserface," Rocket said. Taserface stalked away. "Hey, tell the other guys we said hi, Taserface!"

Taserface paused, then controlled his temper and started walking again. Another Ravager, wearing thick old-fashioned glasses and a long beard, waved the cage holding Groot at Taserface. "Hey, what about this little plant? Can I smash it with a rock?'"

"No," Taserface said. "It's too adorable to kill. Take it to the tailor."

When they were alone, Rocket said to Yondu, "No offense, but your employees are a bunch of jerks."

Yondu was lost in thought for a moment. "I was a Kree battle slave for twenty years until Stakar freed me," he said slowly, remembering. "He offered me a place with the Ravagers, said all I needed to do was adhere to the code. But I was young and greedy and stupid. Like you stealing those batteries."

"That was mostly Drax," Rocket said.

Yondu let the lie pass. "Me and Stakar, the other captains, we weren't so different from you and your friends. The only family I ever had. When I broke the code, they exiled me. This is what I deserve."

"Slow down, drama queen," Rocket said. "You might deserve this, but I don't. We gotta get out of here."

"Where's Quill?"

"He went off with his old man."

"Ego."

"Yeah, it's a day for names," Rocket said. Yondu chuckled. "You smiled," Rocket added, "and for a second I got a warm feeling, but then it was ruined by those disgusting teeth."

Yondu's smile faded.

"Why didn't you deliver Quill to Ego like you promised?" asked Rocket, moving right along.

"He was skinny. Could fit into places we couldn't. Good for thieving," Yondu explained, staring straight ahead.

"Uh-huh." Rocket didn't believe it. There was more to that relationship than Yondu was letting on.

Yondu changed the subject. Clearly, he didn't want to talk about Quill. "I've got an idea on how to get out of here," he said, "but we're gonna need your little friend."

Later that night, Groot wandered through the Ravager ship alone. The Ravagers were mean to him. They yelled in his face, poured drinks on him, made him wear a uniform like theirs. He didn't want any of it.

He wanted to be back with his family.

He heard a voice from around the corner. "*Psst.* Hey, twig, come here. Come on."

It was Yondu, in a barred cell with Rocket.

"Oh man," Rocket said when Groot got closer. "What did they do to you?"

Groot just stood there, looking sad.

"Hey," Yondu said. "You want to help us get out of here?"

Groot nodded.

"There's something I need you to get and bring back to me. In the captain's quarters, there's a prototype fin, like the thing I wore on my head. It's in a drawer next to the bunk. It's red. You got it?"

Groot ran off. Over the next hour he brought them back a pair of Yondu's underwear, a live Orloni, one of the Ravagers' cybernetic eyes, a desk, and a severed toe. Clearly, he was having trouble understanding Yondu's description.

"The drawer you want to open has this symbol on it," Yondu said. He took the Ravager flame patch off his coat and handed it to Groot. Groot took the patch and put it on his head.

"What?" Yondu said. "No!"

"He thinks you want him to wear it like a hat," Rocket explained.

"That's not what I said."

"I am Groot," Groot said.

"He hates hats," Rocket translated.

"I am Groot."

"On anyone, not just himself."

"I am Groot."

"One minute you think someone has a weird-shaped head, the next minute you realize it's because part of it is just the hat." Rocket realized what he'd just said. He looked back at Groot. "That's why you don't like hats?"

Groot nodded.

Frustrated, Yondu snapped, "This is an important conversation right now?"

They sent Groot one more time, and he creeped slowly through the sleeping Ravagers toward a cabinet where he saw the same symbol Yondu had shown him. He extended a vine and pulled the drawer open, then reached in. He pulled out a toy and his face lit up as he looked at it.

Then he jumped as someone behind him said quietly, "That ain't it."

Groot looked over his shoulder and saw Kraglin.

Yondu and Rocket looked up as Kraglin dropped the prototype fin through the bars into the cell. Yondu stared at him coldly. "I didn't mean to do a mutiny," Kraglin said sadly. "They killed all my friends."

After a pause, Yondu said, "Get the Third Quadrant ready for release."

Kraglin gathered himself and thumped his chest in the Ravager salute.

"One more thing," Yondu said as Kraglin turned to go. "Got any clones of Quill's old music on the ship?"

CHAPTER 14

Most of the Ravagers were asleep when Star-Lord's
Awesome Mix Vol. 2 started playing over the ship's
speaker system. The few who were awake went looking
for the source of the music…and one of them walked
into the repair shop where Rocket was just finishing
installing Yondu's new fin.

They grabbed for their weapons, but Yondu was
already whistling.

His arrow punched through the wall and then the
two Ravagers, dropping them where they stood. He

grabbed it as it returned to him, and Rocket picked up the gun one of the Ravagers had dropped.

Together they walked through the ship toward the Third Quadrant, where Kraglin was getting ready for their escape.

In a central observation post, one of the Ravagers spotted them. He ran to the sleeping quarters and woke Taserface. "He's got it! Yondu's got the fin!"

Alarms went off and the Ravagers mobilized. Yondu let the arrow go and started whistling. The arrow left traces of red as it circled and looped through the ship, striking down the Ravagers before they even knew where the escaped prisoners were. They walked out into a central open space ringed by balconies. Ravagers on the balconies started shooting down, but the arrow made short work of them.

Groot spotted one of the Ravagers who'd been mean to him. He screamed in fury and tangled the Ravager's legs in vines. Then Groot threw him off one of the balconies.

They were close to the observation post, where screens showed every part of the ship. Yondu kept whistling, watching the arrow as it streaked across the screens, taking out mutinous Ravagers all over the ship. Rocket finally got in on the act, too, using the screens to aim his gun through the walls and blast away at Ravagers who got too close. Before long, the only Ravager left standing was Taserface. Yondu whistled the arrow at him with a little smile. At the end of the whistle, he added a note and the arrow burst into flame, speeding up and showing the new capabilities of the prototype fin.

Taserface saw it coming and dodged—or at least that's what he thought. But Yondu had let him get out of the way. The flaming arrow punched into a fuel tank behind Taserface, igniting a giant explosion that blew the Ravager across the room.

"You maniac!" Rocket shouted. "The whole ship's gonna blow."

Explosions started tearing the Ravager ship apart, but Yondu didn't look worried. "Not the whole ship," he said. They strode through the burning ship and into the Third Quadrant, where Kraglin almost had it ready for them.

"Release the Quadrant!" Yondu said when they were aboard.

"Aye, Cap'n," Kraglin said. He touched a series of

controls and the forward part of the Ravager ship detached from the rest. Kraglin fired the engines and the Third Quadrant moved clear of the explosions ripping through the main body of the ship.

In the heart of the inferno, Taserface staggered to his feet and reached a wall terminal. He punched in the code to contact the Sovereign. A golden face appeared on the screen. "Who is this?"

"I am sending you the coordinates for Yondu's ship," Taserface said. Behind him, the flames were getting closer. "I only ask one thing: that your high priestess tell him the name of the man what sealed his fate." He paused dramatically. "Taserface!"

The Sovereign officer couldn't help it. She started to laugh.

A moment later, the Ravager ship disintegrated in a giant fireball.

From the pilot's seat, Kraglin aimed the Third Quadrant toward the nearest jump point. "Where to, Cap'n?"

"Ego," Rocket said. He was already punching in the coordinates.

"No, boy!" Yondu protested, but it was too late. The

Third Quadrant passed through the jump portal. Then through another, and another, and another.

"It ain't healthy for the mammalian body to do more than fifty jumps at a time!" Yondu yelled over the roar of the jumps.

"I know that!" Rocket shouted back.

Yondu was looking at the navigation chart. "We're about to do seven hundred!"

The Third Quadrant streaked on, jump after jump, and everyone on board started to feel the effects. Moving through holes in space-time distorted their bodies, stretched them and compacted them. They felt like they were flying apart into tiny pieces, being smashed flat, and stretched like rubber bands all at the same time. *How many more jumps do we have?* Rocket thought.

He looked at the navigation chart through eyes that felt like balloons and realized they had a long way to go.

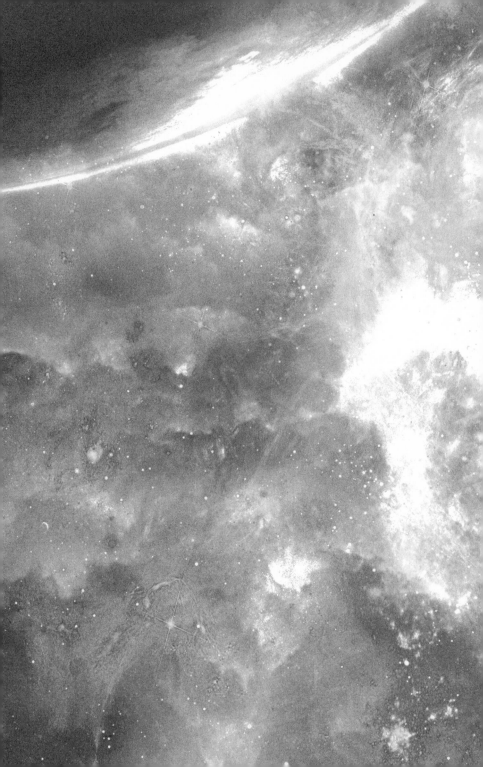

CHAPTER 15

Riding high from his game of catch with Ego—and the dawning realization that his origin was truly extraordinary—Peter stood on a palace balcony looking out over the fabulous gardens of Ego's planet. "So I guess this could all be mine someday," he mused to Gamora. He had music playing, a classic.

Gamora was trying to find out where Rocket was. She had a transmitter and had been calling him every hour or so, but hadn't gotten a response. Now she tried again. "Rocket? Rocket, are you there?"

Static crackled from the transmitter and she gave up. Peter walked up and put an arm around her. "What are you doing, Peter?"

"Dance with me," he said. The music had him feeling romantic. He was half Celestial; he could create energy with his hands; he could hold an Infinity Stone! Life was grand.

"I'm not going to dance with you," she said.

"This is one of the greatest Earth singers of all time." He put her hand on his shoulder and started moving, and she began to dance with him. At first she looked uncertain, but he twirled her gently out and back, and she warmed to it. Now she was looking steadily into his eyes. "Drax thinks you're not a dancer," he said.

"If you ever tell anyone about this," she answered, "I will kill you."

He paused. "When are we going to do something about this unspoken thing between us?"

"What unspoken thing?"

"This…'guy and a girl on a TV show who dig each other but never say anything because if they do the ratings would go down' sort of thing."

Gamora had no idea what he was talking about. She

never did when he talked about Earth stuff. "There's no unspoken thing," she said.

"Well, it's a catch-22," he pointed out. "Because if you said it, then it would be spoken and you'd be a liar, so by not saying anything you are telling the truth and admitting that there is."

"No, that's not what I've—" She pushed him away. "What we should be discussing right now is...something about this place. It doesn't feel right." She walked back inside.

Well, that killed the mood, Peter thought. He followed her. "What are you talking about? You're the one who wanted me to come here!"

"That girl, Mantis. She's afraid of something."

"Why are you trying to take this away from me?" Peter was starting to get upset. Did she not see how important this was to him? How awesome it was to find his father after more than thirty years of missing him?

"I'm not trying—"

"He's my father. He's blood."

"You have blood on Earth," she said. "You never wanted to return there."

"Again, you made me come here! And Earth is the place where my mother died in front of me."

Gamora had no tolerance for the way people fooled themselves sometimes, and she wasn't going to let Peter get away with it now. "No, it's because that place was real, and this place is a fantasy."

"This place is real! I'm only half human, remember?"

"That's the half I'm worried about."

"Oh, I get it," he said. "You're jealous because I'm part god, and you liked it when I was the weak one."

"You were insufferable to begin with," she said. She gave up on the conversation. "I haven't been able to reach Rocket. I'm going to go outside and try to get a signal."

"You know what?" he called after her. "This is the show where one person is willing to open themselves up to new possibility, and the other person is a jerk who doesn't trust anybody! It's a show that doesn't exist, because it would get zero ratings!"

She spun around.

"I finally found my family! Don't you understand that?" he yelled, desperate to break through to her.

He saw this had hurt her, and at first he didn't know why. Then she quietly said, "I thought you already had."

Gamora walked away from the palace out into the countryside, to get her feelings sorted out and get away from Peter for a while. He was so smitten with the idea of this perfect place that he couldn't see the obvious problems, and talking about it more would only make him angry.

She was angry, too. He was making her feel things she had sworn never to feel because they might make her weak. Some tall grass nearby rustled in a sudden breeze, and in a fit of irritation she slashed it down with her sword.

Then, with the rustling gone, she heard another sound. Thrusters.

Gamora stood up and turned to see. Was it Rocket? Had he fixed the *Milano* already?

It wasn't Rocket. It was a small fighter ship, shaped like an arrowhead, with blaster cannons under both wings. And it was coming in fast and low—not a landing path but a strafing approach.

As soon as Gamora had that thought, the ship opened fire.

The ground around her erupted with the blaster impacts. She turned and ran, looking for a place where she wouldn't be exposed. This part of the surface of Ego's planet was riddled with dramatic features: deep canyons and steep ridges. She aimed for the nearest canyon and dove into it just as the fighter screamed overhead, low enough that it would have taken off Gamora's head if she'd still been standing.

"Psychopath!" she screamed. She'd gotten a glimpse of the cockpit and seen a familiar bald, blue head inside. Nebula had gotten free, somehow grabbed a ship, and now she was making good on her promise to kill Gamora.

The fighter came around for another pass, blasting rocks from the walls of the canyon. Gamora ducked into a cave, breathing hard, thinking she was safe... but when she looked outside, she saw Nebula swooping around for another pass.

Gamora ran as Nebula piloted the ship straight into the cave, snapping off pieces of its wings against the walls. She was still firing and still revving the thrusters even as huge chunks of the ship broke off from the cave walls and stalactites. Rocks fell around Gamora and she fell, too, skidding on the stone as Nebula's ship scraped overhead and crashed into the far wall of a chamber. The ship was burning now, and Nebula struggled to free herself from the cockpit.

Under almost any other circumstance, Gamora would have helped. But this was one attempted murder too many. One of the blaster cannons lay on the cave floor, broken free of its wing housing. Gamora picked it up and spliced two of its wires together so it would fire on its own. Then she heaved it up onto her shoulder and took aim.

Cannon fire riddled the ship and shattered the rock formations around it. Gamora didn't stop shooting until the ground beneath Nebula's ship collapsed and the fighter disappeared into a lower chamber. She dropped the cannon and looked down. The burning ship hung upside down in a deep part of the cave. Nebula was still trapped in the cockpit.

I could leave her, Gamora thought. And once she might have. But she wasn't an assassin anymore. Now she was a Guardian of the Galaxy.

She dropped down into the lower chamber and pulled Gamora free of the cockpit just as the ship exploded, flinging them both across the cave. They landed close to each other. Gamora was stunned for a moment. As she tried to get up, she looked over at Nebula, who had broken several bones in the crash. But Thanos had built a healing factor into her, and Nebula reknit her broken bones and straightened her twisted joints in just a few seconds.

Then she came after Gamora again.

"Are you kidding me?!" Gamora screamed. They grappled on the cave floor—not a smooth martial arts fight but a pure emotional fight to the death. Fueled by her hatred, Nebula got a knife to Gamora's throat. She held it there, keeping her sister at her mercy for a long moment. Then she smiled and dropped the knife. "I win," she said. "I win. I bested you in combat."

"No, I saved your life," Gamora said.

"Well, you were stupid enough to let me live."

What? What had Nebula just done? "You let *me* live!" Gamora said.

"I don't need you always trying to beat me!"

"I'm not the one who just flew across the universe just because I wanted to win!"

"Do not tell me what I want."

Gamora waved at the flaming wreckage of Nebula's ship. "I don't need to tell you. It's obvious!"

"You were the one who wanted to win. I just wanted a sister!" Nebula paused, as if she regretted admitting this. Gamora was shocked. She didn't know what to say. "You were all I had," Nebula went on slowly, as if she had to tear each word free of some deep place in her heart. "You were the one who needed to win. Thanos pulled my eye from my head and my brain from my skull and my arm from my body because of you."

They sat in silence for a while after that, two sisters realizing just how much time they had lost. *I needed a sister, too*, Gamora thought. *I didn't want to be the one who always won...but if I hadn't, Thanos would have done to me what he was already doing to Nebula.*

That was in the past. Could they let it stay there, now that Nebula seemed to have gotten the killing urge out of her system? Gamora hoped so. Lost in thought, her sister silent beside her, she noticed a bright-blue light shining from down a cave passage. "What's that?" she wondered aloud.

Maybe it's a way out, she thought. They headed in that direction.

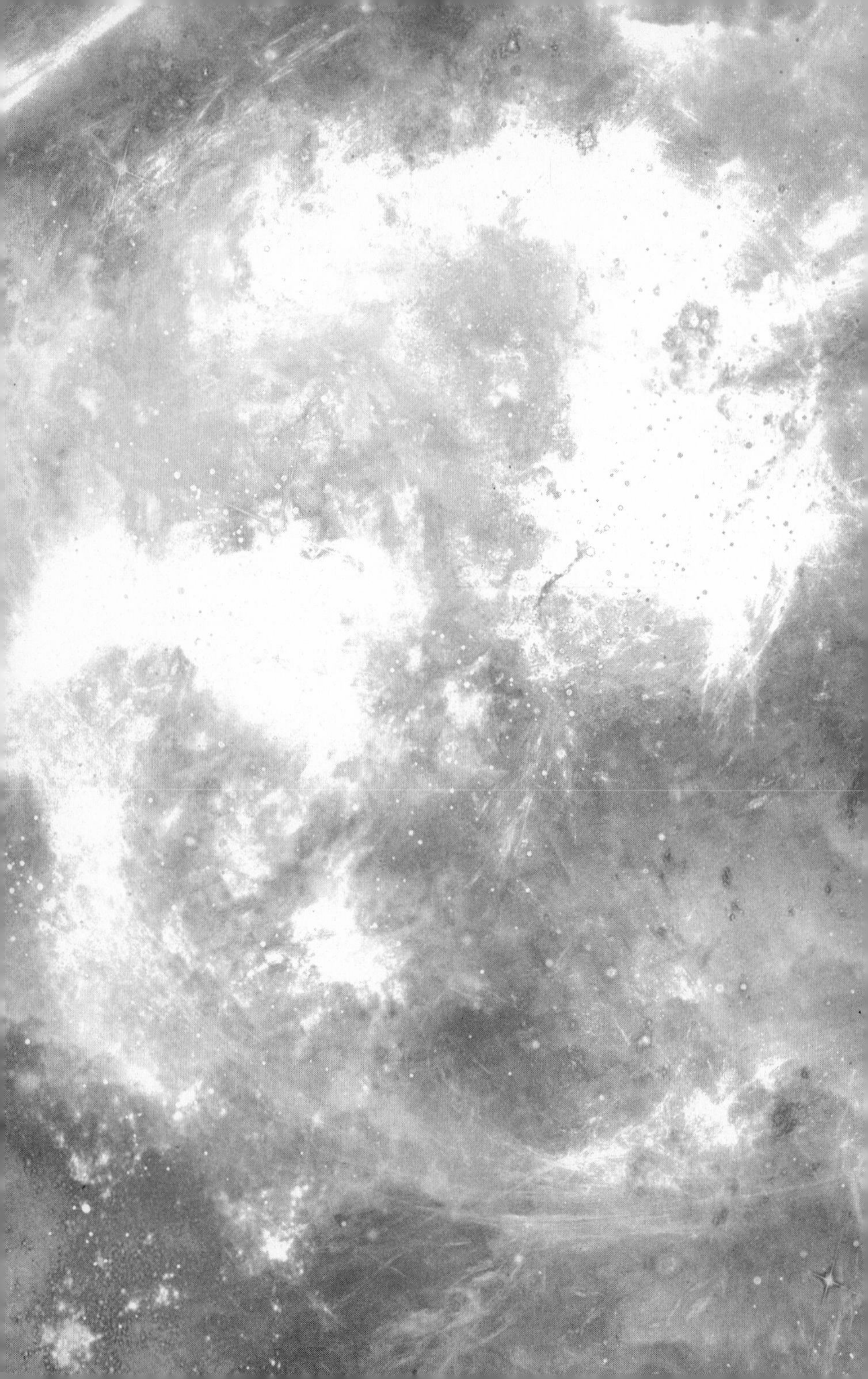

CHAPTER 16

After his talk with Gamora, Peter had retreated to his room and sat by himself, looking out the window and listening to Awesome Mix Vol. 2 on repeat. The tape had reached Meredith and Ego's special song for the fourth time when Ego appeared in the doorway. "You all right, son? I saw your girl stomp off earlier, in quite a huff."

"Yeah," Peter said.

Ego heard the music. "It's fortuitous, you listening to this song."

Peter perked up.

"A favorite of your mom's," Ego explained.

"Yeah. Yeah, it was."

"One of Earth's greatest musical compositions," Ego said. "Perhaps its very greatest."

"Yeah," Peter agreed. Ego definitely understood him. He understood everything Peter felt. This was what Gamora couldn't see.

"You know, Peter, you and I, we're the man in that song," Ego said. He started speaking along with the chorus of the song, eventually explaining what he was driving at. "He loves the girl, but that's not his place. History calls upon great men, and sometimes we are deprived of the pleasures of mortals." Ego had crossed the room to Peter while he spoke. Now they stood together near the window.

"Well, you may not be mortal," Peter said, "but me—"

"No, Peter. Death will remain a stranger to both of us, as long as the light burns within the planet."

Wait, Peter thought. *Seriously?* "I'm immortal?" Ego nodded. "Really?"

"Yes. As long as the light exists."

"Like, I could use the light to build cool things, like how you made this whole planet?"

Ego smiled at Peter's enthusiasm. "Well, it might take a few million years of practice before you get really good at it, but yes."

Peter excitedly explained his new plans.

"Whatever you want," Ego said, just like any father says to a son with grand dreams.

"I'm gonna make some weird stuff," Peter warned. His gloom about Gamora was lifting. This place was his destiny. He belonged here. For the first time in his life, he belonged.

"But you know, Peter," Ego said, more serious now, "it is a tremendous responsibility. Only we can remake the universe. Only we can take the bridle of the cosmos and lead it to where it needs to go."

He held out his hands. Peter did, too. Blue light blazed to life between them. "Wow," Peter said. It was going to be a long time before he got used to that.

Ego watched him for a moment, then seemed to reach a decision. "Come with me," he said. They walked away together into the palace.

Mantis watched them from the shadows. It was happening, just as it had happened thousands of times before...
but now, maybe at last she could do something about it.
She hurried to Drax's room and woke him up. "Drax!
Drax! We need to talk."

Drax saw her and rolled over. "I'm sorry. I like a woman with some meat on her bones."

"What?" She was confused.

"I tried to let you down easily by telling you I found you disgusting."

He didn't understand why she was there. "No, that's not what..." She paused when she saw him acting like he was about to throw up. "What are you doing?"

"I'm imagining...being with you..." Drax gagged.

"Drax, that's not...I don't like you like that. I don't even like the type of thing you are."

He stopped and looked hurt. "Hey, there's no need to get personal."

"Listen!" she said. They were wasting time. "Ego's

gotten exactly what he wanted. I should have told you earlier. I am stupid. You are in danger."

That got his attention. She began to tell him the story, and now he was listening.

Ego and Peter walked through the grand hall with the holographic dioramas of Ego's life, from his first creation to Meredith Quill's pregnancy.

"Now you need to readjust the way you process life," Ego said. "Everything around us—including the girl—everything is temporary. We are forever."

"Doesn't eternity get boring?"

"Not if you have a purpose, Peter. Which is why you're here. I told you how all those years ago I had an unceasing purpose to find life. But what I did not tell you was how when I finally did find it, it was all so... disappointing. And that is when I came to a profound realization. My innate desire to seek out other life was not so that I could walk among that life. Peter, I have found meaning."

He touched Peter's face and a vision exploded in Peter's head. The endless reach of space and time, filled with millions of stars—no, billions—coming into being and burning themselves out, billions of years flashing by in an instant. The entire cosmos in his mind, in a way he had never before conceived. Peter gasped. "I... see it. Eternity."

Gamora and Nebula had finally reached the end of the passage.

It was not a way out.

It ended in a vast chamber, with a thronelike structure on one end and light shining down from a distant hole in the ceiling. And that light fell on an endless pile of bones. Thousands of them, maybe millions, a hillside of bones that reached far above their heads and extended into the darkness on either side of them.

The skulls of every conceivable alien race, jumbled here together in the cold radiance of Ego's light.

"Oh my God," Gamora said. The truth behind the beauty of his planet was even more monstrous than she could have imagined.

Nebula took it all in for a long moment. Then she said, "We need to get off this planet."

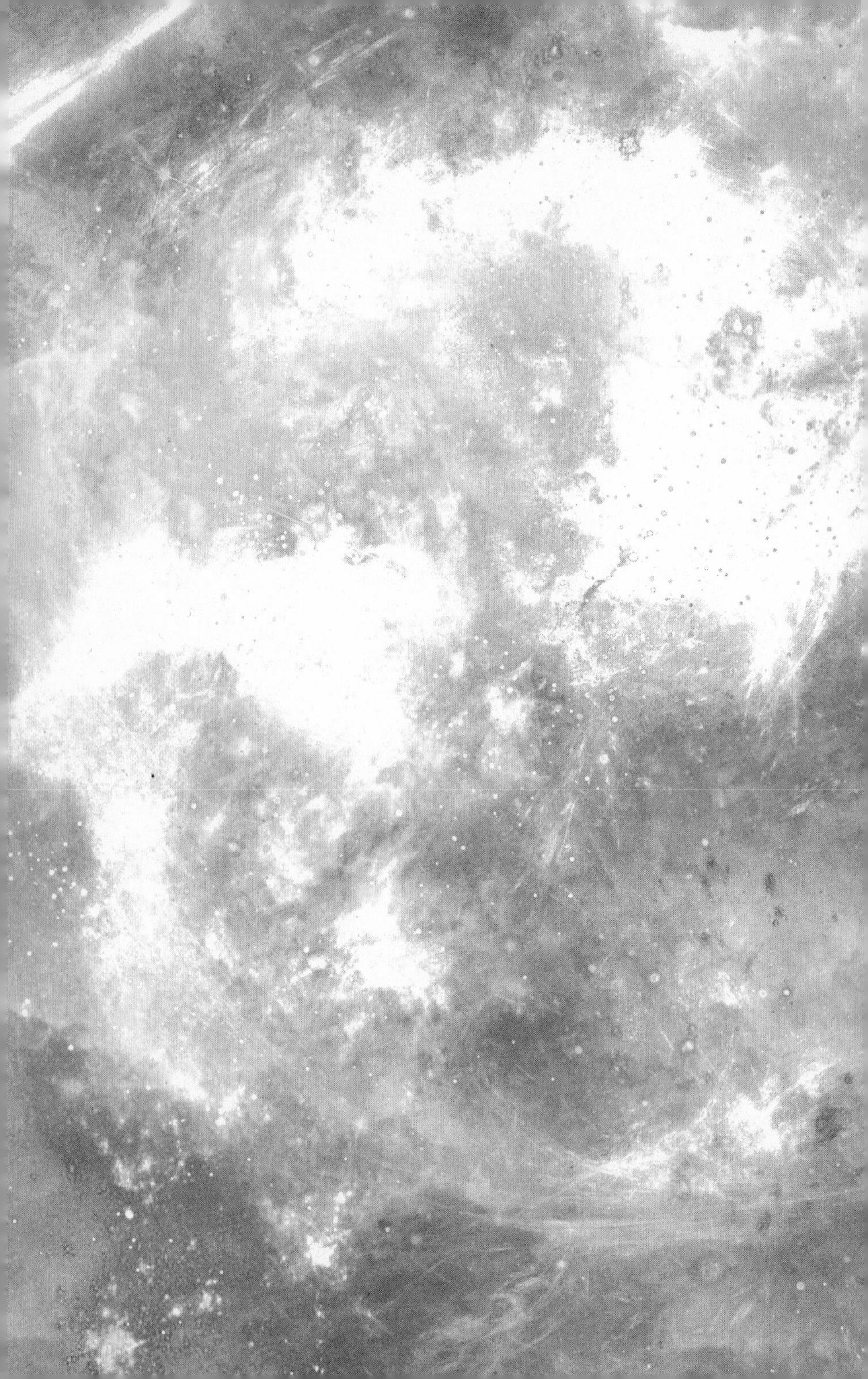

CHAPTER 17

Rocket had long since lost the ability to count the space jumps when the Third Quadrant finally blazed through the last one and slammed into a parking orbit around Ego's planet. It felt bizarre to be back in regular space-time. Rocket looked down at himself to see whether he was normal again. Yondu and Kraglin groaned in their seats. Groot, sitting in his own chair, threw up.

"What you doing, boy?" Yondu demanded when he could speak again.

"I could tell by how you talked about him; this Ego's bad news! We're here to save Quill."

"For what, huh?" Yondu was scornful. "For honor? For love?"

Rocket was up and out of his chair, looking for guns and his bag of bombs. "No, I don't care about those things! I wanna save Quill so I can prove I'm better than him. I can lord this over him forever." Yondu stared, then started laughing. "What are you laughing at me for?"

"You can fool yourself and everyone else, but you can't fool me," Yondu said. "I know who you are."

"You don't know anything about me, loser."

"I know everything about you." Yondu was out of his chair now, too, facing Rocket. "I know you play like you're the meanest and the hardest, but actually you're the most scared of all."

"Shut up," Rocket warned, but Yondu didn't care. He was going to get this sorted out once and for all. If they were going to fight together, they had to drop the masks and admit what they really were.

"I know you steal batteries you don't need, and you

push away anyone who's willing to put up with you," Yondu said, not pulling any punches, "because just a little bit of love reminds you how big and empty that hole inside you actually is."

"I said, shut up! I'm serious, dude." Rocket was just about ready to fight.

Yondu wasn't mad anymore. He was sad, vulnerable. Rocket was amazed to realize that Yondu was actually reaching out to him. Trying to connect.

"Just like my own parents," Yondu said. "Who sold me—their own little baby—into slavery. I know who you are, boy...because you're me."

They stared each other down for a very long, tense moment, with Kraglin watching off to the side, wondering which way things were going to go.

Eventually, Rocket let out a sigh. "What kind of a pair are we?"

"Kind that's about to go fight a planet, I reckon," Yondu said.

"All right. Okay! Good!" Rocket liked the sound of a fight...but when Yondu's words sank in, he paused. "Fight a what?"

After she and Nebula found their way up out of the caves, Gamora raged through Ego's palace until she found Mantis and slammed her up against a wall. "Who are you people? What is this place?"

Drax was also there. "Gamora, let her go."

She ignored him, keeping a grip on Mantis' throat. "The bodies. In the caverns. Who are they?"

Too late, Gamora realized she'd made a mistake by touching Mantis, whose antennae began to glow. "You are scared," she whispered.

Gamora flinched, feeling the emotion intensify. Every fear she'd ever felt was present again. Her stomach knotted up and her heart raced. She dropped Mantis and stepped back. The feeling began to fade, but she could still sense the intensity of it. Her hands surprisingly shook a little.

"What did she do to me?" Gamora said.

Drax was solemn. "She already told me everything."

Nebula and Gamora looked back to Mantis. What was "everything"? Was there more than a secret pile of bones deep in the caves under the planet's surface paradise?

"The bodies are his children," Mantis said slowly.

The meaning of this sank in. If they didn't do something, the bones of Peter Quill would join that pile, and Ego would move on to the next in an infinite roster of children he had sired all across the universe. "We need to find Peter and get off this planet," Gamora said.

"Ego will have found him and won him to his side by now," Mantis said. "He has a way."

Impatient, Nebula asked, "Can't we just go?"

"No," Gamora said. "He's our friend."

"All any of you do is yell at each other," Nebula answered. "You're not friends."

"You're right," Drax said, pausing to consider his words. "We're family." He looked at Mantis, then Gamora. "We leave no one behind." Then, with a look back at Nebula, he added, "Except maybe you."

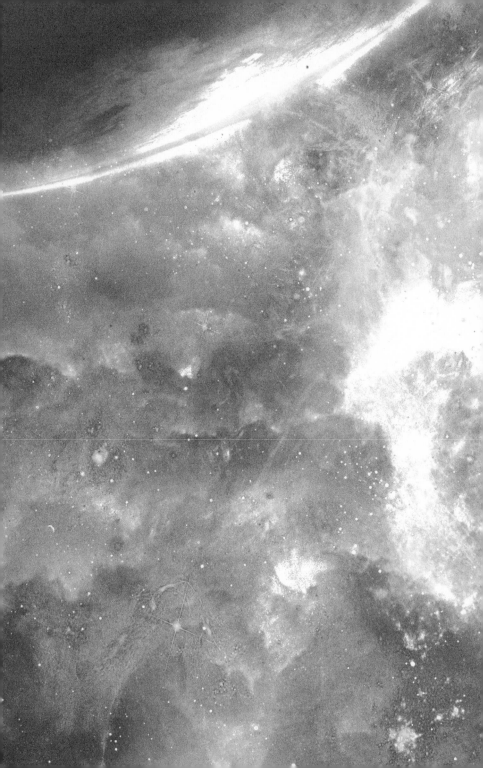

CHAPTER 18

In the open space of the great hall, Ego created a
hologram of endless planets, all lit with the blue energy
of his essence. "I call it the Expansion," he said. "It is my
purpose, and now it is yours as well."

Mind still filled with the cosmic vision, Peter said,
"It's beautiful."

"Over thousands of years I implanted thousands of
extensions of myself on thousands of worlds," Ego said.
One of the display holograms showed him sowing a
radiant plant that took root and spread his blue essence

down into the planet. "I need to fulfill life's one true purpose: to grow and spread, covering all that exists until everything is...me."

The planets in the hologram transformed, becoming shining blue spheres.

All identical. All Ego.

"I only had one problem," Ego went on. "A single Celestial doesn't have enough power for such an enterprise. But two Celestials...now that might just do." The closest display now showed Ego's human form embracing an endless series of aliens, just as Peter had seen him embracing Meredith Quill. "Out of all my labors, the most beguiling was the attempt to graft my DNA with that of another species. I hoped such a coupling would be enough to power such an Expansion. I had Yondu deliver some of them to me. It broke the Ravager code, but I compensated him generously, and to ease his conscience, I said I'd never hurt them. And that was true. They never felt a thing. But one after the other, they failed me. Not one of them carried the Celestial genes...until you, Peter. Out of all my spawn, only you carry the connection to the light."

Ego threw his head back and his voice echoed from

the vaulted ceiling. "For the first time in my existence, I am truly *not* alone!"

Peter blinked and the vision of the cosmos receded a little. It was still there, a vast sensation that a normal human mind could not have comprehended…but part of him was human, and that part mattered, too.

Ego saw the change in Peter. "What is it, son?"

"My friends," Peter said.

"Well, you see. That's the mortal in you, Peter." Ego sounded dismissive.

"Yes."

"We are beyond such things."

Maybe you are, Peter thought. *But I don't think I am. At least not yet.* "But my mother," he said. "You said you loved my mother."

"And that I did. My river lily, who knew all the words to every song that came over the radio. I returned to Earth to see her three times, and I knew if I returned a fourth, I'd never leave. The Expansion—the reason for my very existence—would be over, so I did what I had to do." Ego paused. His voice was full of regret as he gazed up at the glimmering blue array of planets. "But it broke my heart to put that tumor in her head."

The vision of the cosmos vanished from Peter's mind. He replayed Ego's words to himself. *Put that tumor in her head.* "What?"

Ego turned away from the vision of the Expansion to Peter. "All right, I know that sounds bad—"

Peter drew both of his pistols and lit up Ego with a barrage, firing until he had blasted away most of Ego's upper torso. Where the blasters had destroyed Ego's physical body, a skeleton of blue energy remained. Peter kept firing, as if each shot were venting a little of the shock and fury he felt, but Ego withstood the barrage without going down. Peter stopped firing. He still seethed from the betrayal, but he couldn't kill Ego with his pistols. He had never hated someone this much in his life.

Ego, half his head still human and the other half a flickering blue plasma skull, looked at Peter and said, "Who do you think you are?"

"You killed my mother!"

"I tried so hard to find the form that suited you," Ego raged. He transformed until he was a dead ringer for Peter's fantasy father. "And this is the thanks I get?"

Then he was Ego again, fully restored and his face contorted with rage. "You really need to grow up."

Peter was shocked to realize that Ego had never really cared about his mother. She was just a means to an end for him. All his romantic talk about his river lily, it was all a lie. Peter couldn't get a grip on how quickly he whiplashed from joy to betrayal. While Peter grappled with the huge emotions, Ego raised a tendril of energy from the back of the hall and curled it down to spear his son through the back.

Peter spasmed and twisted on the end of the tendril. "I wanted to do this together," Ego growled. "But I suppose you'll have to learn by spending the next thousand years as a battery!"

Not long after they got themselves sorted aboard the Third Quadrant, Rocket heard Gamora's voice over the comm. "Finally! Rocket!"

"Keep that transmitter close by so I can find you," Rocket answered. "I've got an old piece of construction equipment Yondu once used to slice open the Bank of Azkaveri."

Yondu had explained Ego's secret to him, and from the sound of it, Gamora and the gang down on the planet were in the know now, too. Maybe Mantis had told them. Gamora started to explain. "Ego's—"

"I know," Rocket said. "Get ready."

Kraglin punched the release switch and the small drilling vessel dropped away from the Third Quadrant. Yondu gunned it toward Ego's planet, which was no longer a smooth sphere with pockets of brilliant blue.

Now it looked like Ego's angry face.

CHAPTER 19

Peter hung in the air, impaled on the spike of Ego's energy. Ego walked up to him and took his tape player. Peter tried to resist but couldn't. Ego pressed play and the music that Peter's mother had loved filled the room. Ego quoted the lines along with the music. He raised the hand holding the tape player, taking in the vast holographic vision of the Expansion. "Peter. This is the sea."

Ego clenched his fist, crushing the tape. The song cut off and blue Celestial energy flashed out of Peter's body, streaking down into the center of the planet. He felt it reach the planet's core, Ego's pure essence. His Celestial power merged with Ego's and the core flashed a blinding white. Peter could see the entire universe at once again, the cosmic vision returning to show him the beginning of the Expansion. All across the universe, the plants Ego had rooted exploded into monstrous, scintillating blobs of life. The ice cream shop in Missouri where Meredith Quill had kissed her spaceman, way back in 1980, was crushed by the spreading blue. On other planets, the same thing happened. Heaving masses of blue Celestial essence overwhelmed cities and spread over remote landscapes. Terrified people watched or ran, unable to believe what they were seeing.

Back in the great hall, Ego leaned his head back and smiled. The Expansion! At last it was happening....

With a crash, Drax interrupted him by kicking in the great hall's main door. Ego glared in his direction, energy crackling around his body, but before he could do anything, Yondu's drilling ship smashed through the palace roof.

"Hey there!" Yondu sang out—and a split second

later the ship crashed down on Ego, driving him into the floor with a boom that shook the room's mighty pillars.

The tendril of energy holding Peter disappeared and he fell to the floor. Gamora ran to help him. "I told you something didn't feel right."

"'I told you so'? That's what I need to hear right now?"

"I came back, didn't I?"

"Because there's an unspoken thing," he said as he got to his feet.

"There is no unspoken thing," she said firmly, and dragged him toward the ship.

Drax and Mantis were already climbing on board. Groot waved as they approached. "You could have killed us all!" Drax said when he saw Rocket.

Rocket looked annoyed. "*Uhh*, 'thank you, Rocket'?"

"We had it under control," Drax complained.

"We do not," Mantis said. "That is only an extension of his true self. He will be back soon."

Rocket noticed Nebula and glared at her. "What's she doing here?"

"Whatever I have to do to get a ride home," she said, returning the glare.

He appealed to Gamora. "She tried to murder me."

"I saved you, you stupid fox."

"He's not a fox," Gamora said.

"I am Groot," Groot said.

"I'm not a raboon, either!" Rocket yelled.

Groot corrected him. "I am Groot."

"Raccoon, whatever."

Outside, the floor shattered as more tentacles of brilliant blue burst upward from the planet's core. Ego was back. "How do we kill the Celestial?" Drax asked.

"There's a center to him," Peter said. "His brain, his soul, whatever it is. It's in a protective shell."

"It's in the caverns below the surface," Mantis said.

The tentacles wrapped around Yondu's ship. He gunned the thrusters and fought them as Peter came into the cockpit and saw him. "Yondu?!"

"Thrusters are out," Yondu said, by way of greeting.

Peter sat in the other pilot's seat and popped the cover off the navigation console. He saw wires that had jerked loose in the crash and started stripping them so he could wire them back together. "Guess I should be glad I was a skinny kid. Otherwise you'd have delivered me to this maniac."

The columns of the great hall cracked and started to shift as Ego's tentacles pulled the ship down through the floor. "You still think that's the reason I kept you around?" Yondu couldn't believe it.

"That's what you told me," Peter said.

"Well, once I figured out what happened to them other kids, I wasn't just gonna hand you over."

Peter kept working on the wires. "You said you were gonna eat me!"

"That was being funny!"

"Not to me!"

"You people have issues," Rocket commented.

"Well, of course I have issues," Peter said. He pointed out the window, where the humanoid energy skeleton of Ego was re-forming. "That's my freakin' father!"

Peter got the wires spliced together and the ship's thrusters roared to life. He took the controls and powered the ship straight ahead.

It plowed through Ego's spectral form and smashed through a huge circular window out into the open sky. Then it dove down to ground level.

"We should be going up!" Yondu said.

"Can't," Peter said. "Ego wants to eradicate the universe as we know it. We have to kill him. Rocket!"

"Got it!" Rocket flipped a switch and dozens of tiny spheres rolled on tracks across the ship's hull. They arranged themselves into a pattern on its nose and activated. A slashing pattern of lasers drilled through the rocks and earth below them, making a path for the ship as it descended into the planet's interior. When they got to the caverns, the lasers refocused on tunnels, blasting them open before the ship got there.

"Woo-hoo!" Peter whooped. He couldn't help himself. If you couldn't enjoy moments like this, life wasn't worth living.

"So we're saving the galaxy again?" Rocket wondered. While he talked, Rocket kept the lasers calibrated and aimed to clear a passage for the ship.

"I guess," Peter said.

"Awesome. We're really going to be able to jack up our price if we're *two*-time galaxy savers."

"I seriously can't believe that's where your mind goes."

"It was just a random thought, man, I thought we

were friends! Of course I care about the planets and the buildings and all the animals on the planets."

"And the people," Peter reminded him.

Rocket shrugged. *"Ehhhh."*

"The crabby puppy's so cute," Mantis said in a high-pitched voice and with a delighted smile. "He makes me want to die!"

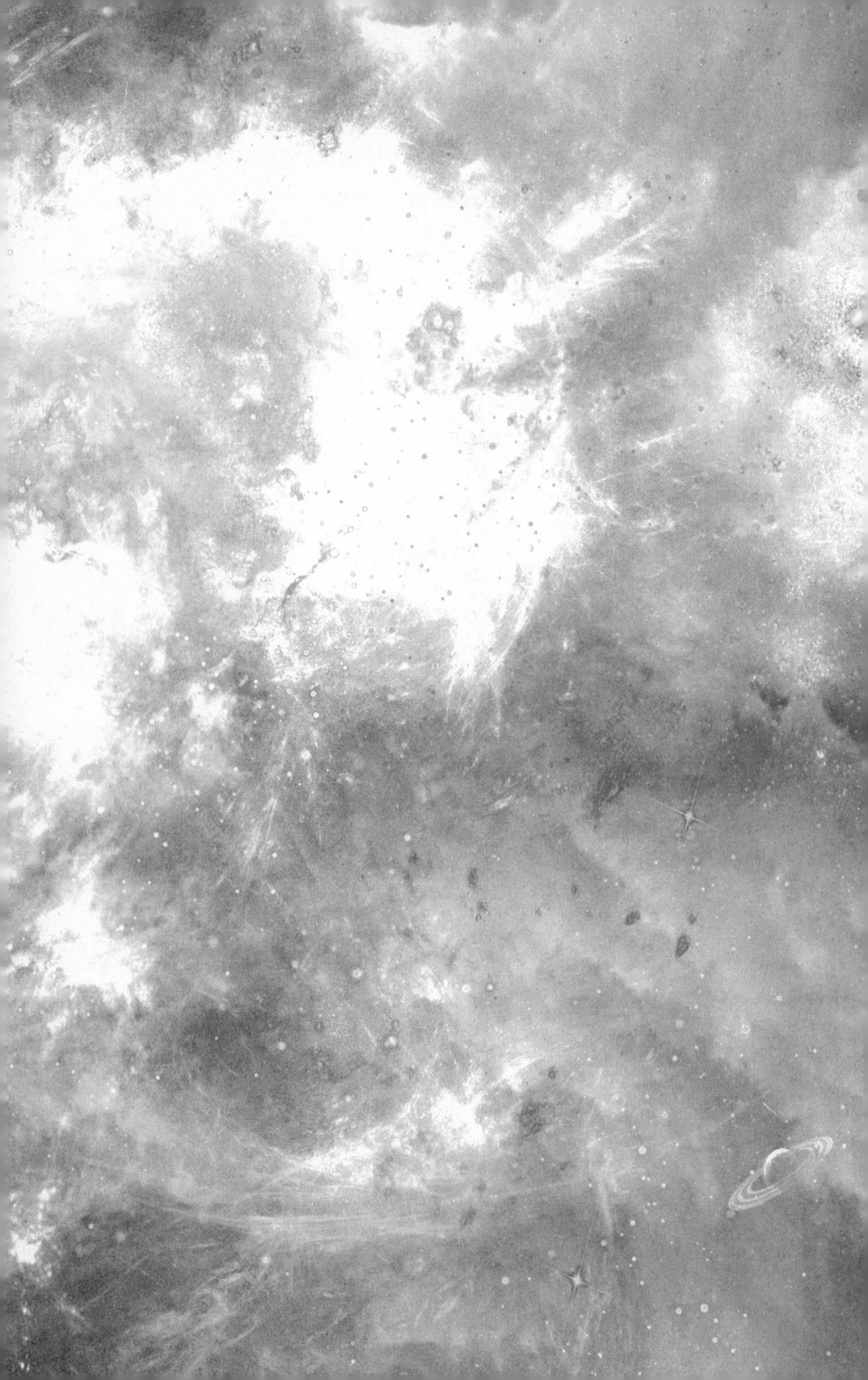

CHAPTER 20

Aboard the Third Quadrant, Kraglin sat listening to music and eating, waiting for his orders from Yondu. Then he looked up when he saw flashes from near the jump point. His eyes bugged out. The flashes were Sovereign ships. A lot of them.

He tried to raise Yondu on the comm, but Yondu didn't answer.

"So tell me," Yondu said over the thunderous noise of the lasers destroying rocks, "why'd Ego want you here?" He knew Ego had some lunatic plan, but he had never known all the details.

"He needs my genetic connection to the light to help destroy the universe," Peter explained, knowing it sounded crazy. "He tried to teach me how to control the power."

"So could you?"

"A little. I made a ball."

"A ball?" Yondu sounded disappointed.

"I thought as hard as I could," Peter protested. "It was all I could come up with."

"You *thought*. You think when I make this arrow fly I use my head?"

The ship crashed and scraped through the last narrow passage, tearing away part of its hull. Then it floated into the immense central cavern at the heart of Ego. Thick, curving stalks of stone converged on the essence of Ego himself, a crackling blue sphere protected by a thick wall of ore.

Mantis looked out the window. "There. That's Ego's core."

"That ore is thick, Rocket," Gamora said.

"I got it covered," said Rocket. He tapped keys and rocked a joystick around. On the ship's hull, the laser spheres moved into a tight circular pattern. They fired as one, starting to cut through the protective wall to Ego's core.

"We must hurry," Mantis warned. "It will not take Ego long to find us."

"Keep it steady," Rocket said.

"If we drill into the center, we kill him," Peter said.

Molten ore began to drip around the hole formed by the lasers. They were getting through, but they weren't there yet.

"Cap'n?" Kraglin's voice came over the comm speaker next to Yondu.

"What is it, Kraglin?"

"Remember that Ayesha chick?"

"Yeah, why?"

"Ummmm..."

Yondu glanced out the side cockpit window. Dozens of Sovereign drones swarmed into the cavern. He shouted and hauled the ship into a fast turn away from the core. The drones peppered the ship with fire. As

Yondu evaded them, he turned the ship on its side—and Drax, Mantis, and Gamora tumbled out through the hole torn in the hull.

They landed on one of the stone formations near the core and looked up at the horde of Sovereign ships chasing Yondu's battered mining vessel.

Inside the ship, Peter was yelling at Rocket. "Why aren't you firing the lasers?!"

Rocket was already coming up with a new plan. He called as he ran toward the rear, "They blew out the generator! I think I packed a small detonator." He found a pack and started rummaging through it.

"A detonator's worthless without explosives," Nebula pointed out.

Rocket held up a handful of the Anulax batteries. "Well, we got these."

"Are those things powerful enough to kill Ego?"

"If it is, it'll cause a chain reaction throughout his entire nervous system." As he spoke, Rocket was cobbling the batteries and detonator together into a bomb.

"Meaning what?"

"The entire planet will explode. We'll have to get out of here fast. I rigged a timer." He and Quill tapped the discs that generated their space suits and Quill covered his face with his Star-Lord mask. Then they jumped out of the ship, with Groot on Rocket's shoulder. They dodged drone fire and skidded to a stop inside the hole the ship's laser had drilled.

Down on the ground, Mantis trembled as blue light began to shine through new cracks below their feet. "He's coming."

"Didn't you say you could make him sleep?" Drax asked.

"When *he* wants. He's too powerful! I can't!"

"You have to believe in yourself," Drax said. "Because I believe in you."

Ego's face appeared in the nearest wall and flared into a brilliant wave of energy. It spread toward them. Mantis looked down. A crack in the ground near her feet shone bright blue as well. She dropped to one knee and thrust a hand into it. "Sleep!" she screamed over the roar of the energy and the battle above them.

The energy vanished into trailing wisps. Mantis looked up, astonished.

Drax, eyes wide, said, "I never thought she'd be able to do it, as weak and skinny as she appears to be."

Her antennae were almost too bright to look at. "I don't know how long I can hold him," she said, straining with effort and urgency.

Rocket shone a flashlight around. The tunnel ended several meters short of the core. There was a small passage forking away from the end of the bored passage. "The metal's too thick," Rocket said. "For the bomb to work, we have to place it on the core. And our fat butts ain't gonna fit through those teeny-tiny holes."

Peter had been in this situation before. Once, he'd been the skinny kid sent through holes too small for an adult to get through. "Well..." he said, and looked at Groot, who was staring off into space.

"That's a terrible idea," Rocket said.

"Which is the only kind of idea we have left."

Rocket growled and got to work. Peter readied his guns and jumped back out into the battle. He had to give Rocket some cover before the Sovereign realized what was happening...or before Ego woke up.

Rocket called Groot over.

"All right; first you flick this switch, then this switch. That activates it. Then you push this button, which will give you five minutes to get outta there." He pointed to another button. "Now, whatever you do, don't push *this* button, because that will set off the bomb immediately, and we'll all be dead. Now repeat back what I just said."

"I am Groot," Groot said.

"Uh-huh."

"I am Groot."

"That's right."

Groot pointed to the detonator button. "I am Groot."

"No!" Rocket yelled. "No, that's the button that will kill everyone! Try again."

Groot looked at the bomb. He went through the first two steps correctly again, then hesitated...and pointed to the detonator button again. "I am Groot," he said proudly.

"No! That's exactly what you just said!" Rocket tried to control his temper, but Groot could be maddening. "How is that even possible? Which button is the button you're supposed to push? Point to it."

Groot pointed to the detonator button.

"No!" Rocket didn't know what to do.

Quill appeared in the mouth of the tunnel. "Hey, you're making him nervous!"

"Shut up and give me some tape. Does anybody have any tape out there? I wanna put some tape over the death button!"

"I don't have any tape!" Quill called back. "Let me check!" He jetted away, and over the sounds of the battle, Rocket heard him yelling to the rest of the team. Soon he was back. "Nobody has any tape!"

"Not a single person has tape?" Rocket found this hard to believe. "Did you ask Nebula?"

"Yes!"

"Are you sure?"

"I asked Yondu and she was sitting right next to him," Quill said.

"I knew you were lying!" Rocket shouted.

"You have priceless batteries and an atomic bomb in your bag!" Quill shouted back. "If anyone is going to have tape, it's you!"

"That's exactly my point! I have to do everything!"

Quill jetted away again, firing at Sovereign drones. Rocket turned back to Groot, figuring he'd just have to try one more time...but the sapling Groot was gone, and so was the bomb.

Echoing back up the tiny passage that led to Ego's core, Rocket heard: "I...am...*Grooooooot!*"

He sighed. "We're all gonna die."

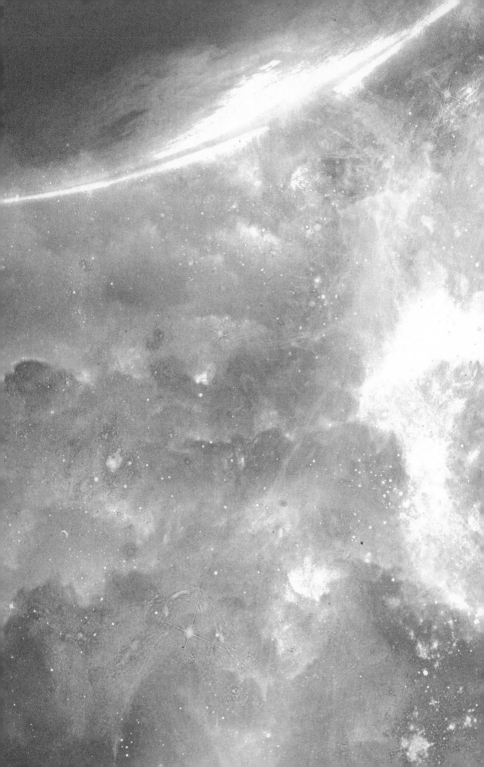

CHAPTER 21

Yondu was trying to evade the Sovereign drones, but the drilling ship wasn't built for quick maneuvering. They were taking a beating. "Thrusters are out again!" he shouted. "We're done for without that generator!"

Nebula triggered a switch on her cybernetic arm. He saw what she was doing and wondered if it would work.

As Nebula wired herself into the ship, High Priestess Ayesha's voice echoed from the speakers of every drone. "Guardians," she announced, "perhaps it will provide you solace that your deaths are not without purpose.

They will further the warning to all those tempted to betray us." Her voice rang through the vast space at the center of Ego's planet. "Don't screw with the Sovereign."

Nebula had herself plugged into the system as a backup generator. "This is gonna hurt," Yondu warned.

"Promises, promises," Nebula said, sneering.

Yondu hit a switch and Nebula screamed. Electricity crackled around her as the ship tapped her like a battery. The ship's lasers came to life, dozens of the tiny spheres spraying laser fire in every direction. Yondu had the targeting software ready, and the lasers annihilated the entire drone fleet, cutting off Ayesha's voice.

Everything was overloaded. Circuits shorted out and energy feedback reached a critical point.

"We're gonna blow!" Yondu yelled.

Down on the ground, Gamora cried out Peter's name as the drilling ship blew apart. Then she saw Nebula falling from the tumbling wreckage and landing safely on the ground. A moment later, Peter and Yondu appeared—Peter hovered using one of Rocket's aero-rigs, and Yondu dangled from his arrow. "Ha," Peter said. "You look like Mary Poppins."

Concerned, Yondu asked, "Is he cool?"

"Yeah, he's cool," Peter said.

"I'm Mary Poppins, y'all!" Yondu yelled as they touched down not far from Gamora.

Mantis, still crouched over the vein of Ego's energy, struggled to keep him from waking up.

A moment later, Rocket touched down next to them. All the Guardians were reunited...except Groot, who they hoped was somewhere near the core with the bomb. It hadn't gone off and killed them all, so things were still going more or less according to plan.

But that luck didn't last. Wreckage crashed down around them from the drilling ship and the shattered swarm of Sovereign drones. A piece struck Mantis, knocking her down and dislodging her hand from the vein of Ego's essence.

"Mantis, look out!" Drax cried, far too late.

The vein brightened, and the brilliance of Ego waking up spread throughout the core. Drax bent over Mantis. "She's just unconscious," he said, picking her up.

But now it would not be long before Ego awoke. They were running out of time.

Peter ran over to Rocket, shouting over the tumult. "How long until the bomb goes off?"

"In the unlikely event that Groot doesn't kill us all, about six minutes."

"Kraglin!" Yondu shouted into a communicator. "We need the Quadrant for an extraction, T minus five minutes!"

"Aye, Cap'n."

"Somebody's gotta be up top when Kraglin arrives," Peter pointed out. Otherwise he wouldn't know where the rendezvous was supposed to be. He slapped his space-suit disc onto Drax's back. "Drax, take Mantis!"

Howling with the pain of the suit harness on his sensitive skin, Drax shot toward the surface. Mantis, still unconscious, dangled from his arms.

And then Ego woke up.

The ground heaved under the Guardians. Gamora slipped and toppled into a hole that opened up under her feet. Peter shouted after her, but she was gone. Blue tentacles of Ego's energy thrust up through the rock, striking at the Guardians. Ego's face appeared in a column of stone, filled with rage. "Peter!" he roared in a voice that made the entire planet tremble.

Nobody had noticed Nebula. Seeing Gamora fall, she had plunged into the pit after her, diving into the open space. She caught her sister just before they both crashed to the floor. Nebula caught the rock wall and held both of them. With a scream of effort, she flung Gamora up onto a ledge and crawled up after her.

For a moment, the sisters glared at each other. Then Nebula panted, "Get over it."

Near the core itself, Ego loomed over Peter. "I know this isn't what you wanted...but what kind of father would I be to let you make this choice?" He was completely deranged, Peter realized. All he could see was his vision. Peter's human emotions didn't matter to Ego. Nothing mattered to Ego but himself.

Yondu whistled his arrow into action. It pierced Ego's stone face a dozen times, eventually breaking it apart into glowing rubble that crashed down around them. Other animated columns of rock trapped Rocket, but he blew them apart with a double handful of the bombs in his pack.

Ego re-formed. "Soon, Peter, we will be all there is. Just stop."

Peter fired with both pistols, deflecting the tentacles and the sweeping columns of rock—but he couldn't hit them all, and in the next moment one of them hit him. He skidded across the ground, coming to rest flat on his back. He lay stunned, his face bloodied, unable to get up.

Below the group, Nebula and Gamora looked up. The surface was a long way off. "We have to get to the extraction point!" Gamora shouted as columns of stone were rising to block access to the surface.

They looked at each other, realizing what they had to do. Together, the sisters sprinted forward and jumped, catching the upper edge of one of the columns. Maybe they could ride it all the way to the surface.

Drax had reached the surface and spotted the Third Quadrant. He ran toward it, carrying the unconscious Mantis. Ahead of him, Kraglin had opened the ship's bay doors.

Then blue tentacles erupted through the earth, wrapping around the ship and dragging it forward and down. Drax skidded to a halt, but he couldn't get out of the way. The ship was about to crush him and Mantis. Drax bent over Mantis to protect her as best he could.

Inside the ship, Kraglin made a desperate lunge for the thrusters and lifted the ship away from the surface, clearing Drax and Mantis by less than a foot. The engines thrummed to full power and the Third Quadrant tore free of Ego's tentacles. Drax stood as the ship swung around to pick them up, but his feet wouldn't move. He looked down and realized he was sinking slowly into the earth. He strained but could not pull free. Slowly he was drawn down, holding Mantis up, until the earth closed over their heads.

Below the surface, the column carrying Nebula and

Gamora suddenly tipped at an angle and smashed into the wall of the cave. They were pinned in the rubble, which rose around them and sealed them away.

And in the deepest part of the core, within sight of Ego's brain, the tunnel began to collapse around Groot.

Peter looked on in horror as a cliff wall near the core ripped itself in half, revealing the pure essence of Ego blazing forth from within. Ego walked out, skeletal and terrifying. He flicked a hand, and a swirl of stones dragged Yondu down to the ground. Rocket was next, disappearing in a swirl of blue and crashing stone. He had blasted free of the tentacles time and again, but Ego was more powerful now in his fury. The tentacles snapped around Rocket in a cage and began to squeeze.

"I told you," Ego said. "I don't want to do this alone." Again, Peter was pierced by tentacles that snapped out from the direction of the core. He fought them, but they held him fast. "You cannot deny the purpose the universe has bestowed upon you!" Ego was assuming his human form again, layer by layer. First bone, then muscle, and last the skin that made him a frightening version of the spaceman Meredith Quill had loved until she died.

As the tentacles tapped Peter Quill's Celestial energies, the planet began to come to life again. And on the other planets where Ego had left his strange plants, the terrible blue life surged into action again, overwhelming everything around it. Peter could feel it, the awful vitality overwhelming cities and sweeping over everything that was not Ego...the Expansion was happening despite all Peter's efforts to stop it.

"It doesn't need to be like this, Peter," Ego called out over the rumbling of shifting rock. "Why are you destroying our chance? Stop pretending you aren't what you are. What greater meaning can a life possibly have to offer?"

Peter felt the call of his destiny again. The surge of Celestial power was seductive, warring with his anger at what Ego had done to his mother. His twin natures, Celestial and human, were at war.

Yondu saw Peter's struggle, and he desperately tried to help. "I don't use my head to fly the arrow, boy! I use my—" Yondu's voice was cut off as the rocks creeped over his face, but Peter knew what he had been about to say.

My heart.

Peter looked over at his father. At the same time he remembered all the times other people had brought him joy. Laughing with his mother. A rare moment when Yondu taught him something that wasn't illegal, and Peter felt like he belonged. Sharing a joke with Rocket, a meal with Gamora, the deep connections he had forged.

Ego had never given him anything like that. In fact, Ego wanted to destroy it. He was out to destroy everything that had ever mattered to his son.

Anger surged through Peter. He clenched his fists and closed his eyes, fighting for the human side of himself...and beginning to reclaim the Celestial energy that was bleeding away into Ego's planet. He felt the power return to him, and realized that his destiny was not human or Celestial.

It was both.

He opened his eyes and saw Ego staring at him in shock. "You shouldn't have killed my mom," he said.

And then he broke free of the tentacles and rode a wave of anger and Celestial power toward his father. He smashed into Ego, driving him through rock walls and pounding at him with his bare fists, shattering rocks on

Ego's head. Every blow exposed the cold, blue essence beneath Ego's human skin.

Staggered by the attack, Ego lost control over the energies of the planet. Drax heaved himself up through the earth, gasping for breath. Gamora and Nebula fought their way to the surface. Rocket exploded out of the tentacle-cage, and Yondu sat up out of his rocky tomb.

Peter sensed the same on all the other planets where Ego was trying to grow. The surging blue life slowed... and stopped. Its light began to dim.

And at the planet's core, Groot struggled to continue on his mission. Ego's core, his self, was within reach.

"Groot!" Rocket yelled from the mouth of the tunnel. "If you can hear me, hurry up! I'm not sure how long Quill can keep him distracted!"

Groot went through the steps. He activated the timer. He pressed the first button to prime the bomb. Then he hesitated. What was he supposed to do next? His finger hovered over one button...and then he changed his mind and pressed the other.

The timer started counting down. 4:59...4:58...

Groot ran.

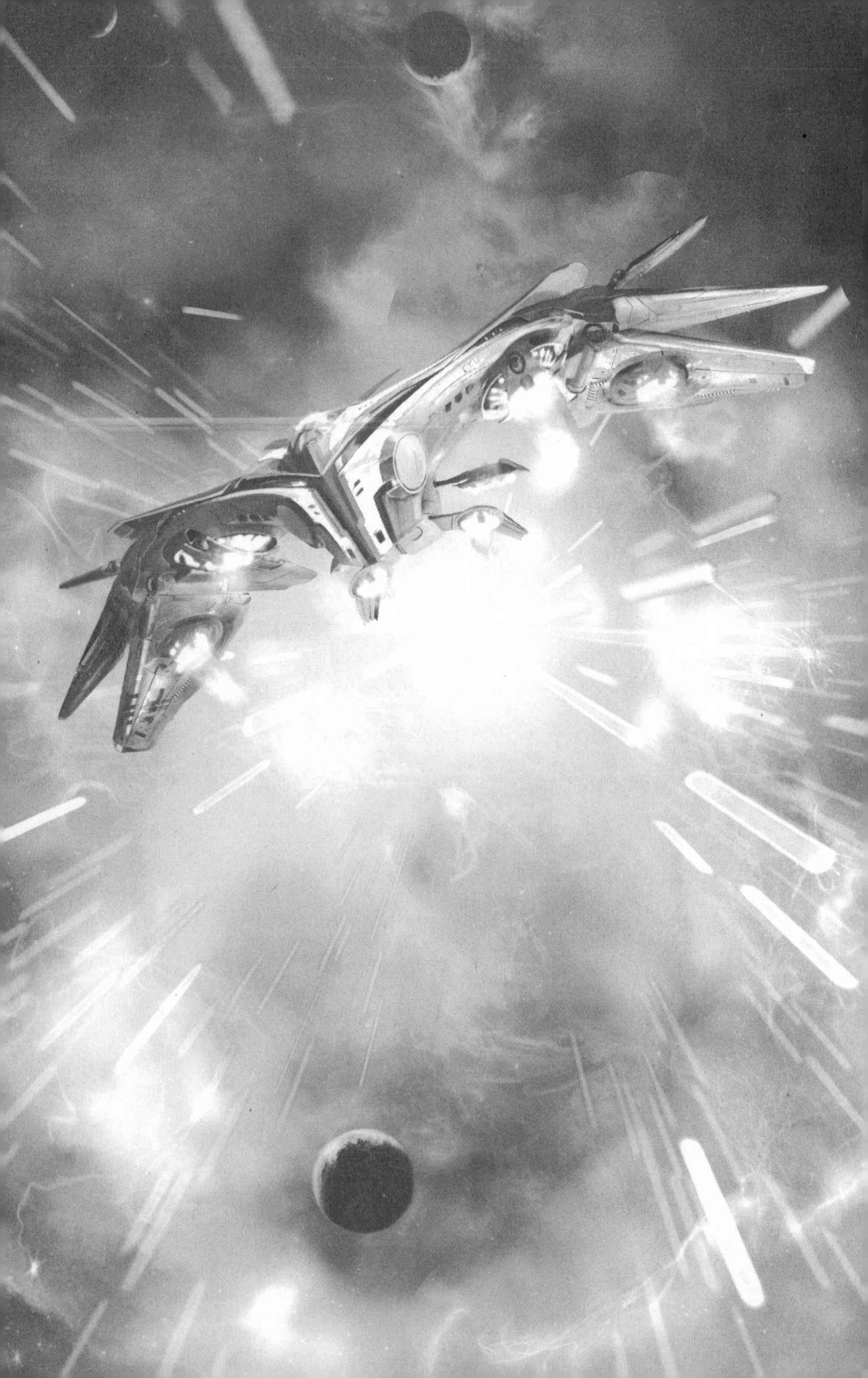

CHAPTER 22

Drax pitched Mantis into the Quadrant and clambered in. Nebula and Gamora were almost to the surface. Rocket, with Groot on his shoulder, flew back toward Yondu, the last of them stuck down in the core with no way out. "Yondu! We're about to blow!"

"Get to the ship!" Yondu called back.

"Not without Quill!"

"You need to take care of the twig!"

Rocket landed and said what he really meant. "Not without you."

Yondu shook his head. "I ain't done nothing right my whole life, rat. You need to give me this."

Rocket knew what Yondu was doing, and knew he wouldn't be able to change Yondu's mind. Someone had to stay behind to get Quill off the planet if he could get free of Ego before the bomb went off. But whoever did that probably would not live to tell the story. Rocket detached two things from his belt. "A space suit and an aero-rig," he said. "I only have one of each."

Yondu took them. Rocket hovered, about to take off. "I am Groot," Groot said.

"What's that?" Yondu asked.

"He said 'welcome to the frickin' Guardians of the Galaxy,'" Rocket said. "Only he didn't use 'frickin'.'"

Yondu nodded. "Bye, twig."

Rocket accelerated upward. "We're gonna need to have a real discussion about your language," he said to Groot.

They got to the Quadrant and landed just inside the open bay door. "Where's Peter?" Gamora demanded. "Rocket, where is he?" Rocket didn't answer. He was looking at his timer. There was less than a minute left.

"Rocket, look at me. Where is he?"

Rocket just shook his head, but Groot pointed back outside.

"No," Gamora said. "No, we're not leaving him now." She grabbed a rifle and started to head out onto the surface again—but sparks of blue light flared around her and she dropped, senseless, to the deck.

"I'm sorry," Rocket said, still holding the stun gun he'd used to stop her. "I can only afford to lose one friend today."

He looked up toward the Quadrant's cockpit. "Kraglin, go!"

Kraglin reached for the thruster controls, but Drax stopped him. "No, wait." He leaned down to the intercom. "Rocket. Where's Quill?"

Rocket didn't answer.

"Where's Quill?" Drax shouted in anguish. The Quadrant lifted away from the surface. Rocket stared out the closing door. There was nothing any of them could do. The fate of the universe was at stake, and only some of them were going to survive.

Deep inside the planet, Ego had regained the upper hand after his son's initial surprise attack. He and Peter charged at each other again and again, only now Peter was playing defense because Ego had figured out Rocket's plan. He knocked Peter down and struggled toward the bomb. The rock walls had fallen away from around the core and the bomb was visible on Ego's pulsing brain. "No!" Ego shouted. "We need to stop it!"

Peter tackled him and shoved him away from the core.

"Stop it! Listen to me!" Ego said. He was no longer fighting, just trying to talk. "You are a god."

Peter looked at his father, his immortal father. He had tried everything in his power to sacrifice Peter just like he had sacrificed all his other children. He had nearly made Peter into an instrument to destroy the universe. He had told Peter none of his friends mattered.

He had killed Peter's mother.

And now he was afraid.

"If you kill me," Ego said, "you'll be just like everybody else."

You really don't get it, Peter thought.

"What's so wrong with that?" Star-Lord asked.

For the first time, Ego understood his son. "No!" he cried out again...and then the bomb went off.

The explosion of the Anulax batteries destroyed the core of Ego's self, setting off a chain reaction that spread through the planet's interior. The human form of Ego crumpled in on itself and turned to dust before Peter's eyes. The last vestiges of the Celestial energy flickered in the palms of his hands and went out. *I killed my father*, Peter thought. *Because he killed my mother; because he would have drained me and cast me aside; because he would have annihilated all my friends without a second thought.*

But it still wasn't easy to think about.

Peter watched the planet begin to collapse around him, knowing he was about to die in the rolling waves of fire that spread from the destroyed core...and then Yondu burst into view and snatched him up.

They streaked toward the surface, flying up through a seam in the rock as a column of fire rose below them. As they jetted higher into the atmosphere, Yondu turned to Peter. "He may have been your father, boy, but he wasn't your daddy. I'm sorry I didn't do nothing right."

He slapped the space-suit disc onto Peter's shoulder and the suit flickered to life. They were in the upper atmosphere now, surrounded by the swirl of electromagnetic energies between the air and the hard vacuum of space. Still they flew higher.

"What?" Peter looked down and saw the planet collapsing into itself. Then he looked back at Yondu, who looked straight ahead, a smile on his face as they reached space. Yondu didn't have a space suit. He had one of Rocket's aero-rigs on his back, but nothing to protect him from the vacuum. Peter understood what was happening. "Yondu, what are you doing? You can't do this!"

Yondu still looked up. The aero-rig sputtered and went out. Now they were moving only from momentum, flying through the empty space near the self-destructing ruin of Ego's planet.

"Yondu! No!" Peter slapped at the disc, thinking maybe he could get it to protect both of them—but it was already too late for Yondu. Looking Peter in the eye, he put both hands on the sides of Peter's face. Frost creeped over his blue skin. He held Peter's gaze and gave his cheek a fatherly pat. Then his arms went limp and the frost creeped over his eyes.

All Peter could do was hold him, knowing Yondu had sacrificed his life to get him off the planet. It was true. Yondu had been the only real father Quill had ever known, and now he was gone.

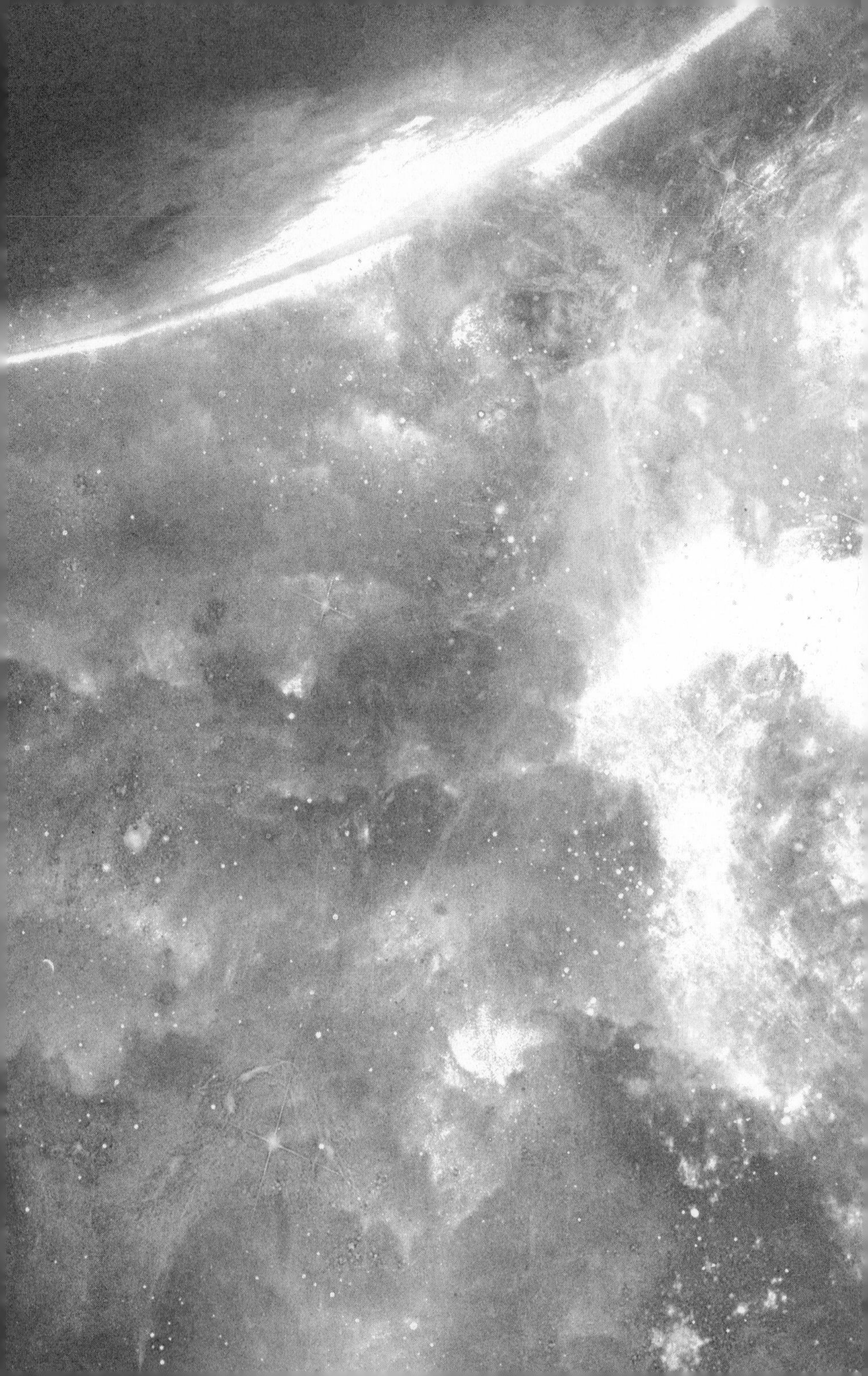

CHAPTER 23

They prepared Yondu's body in the Ravager way, laying him on a pallet and putting mementos and gifts on it next to him. Peter placed a doll that Yondu had cherished since Peter was a child. The other Guardians added insignia, bits of cloth with badges and medallions, other things that meant something to them. Mantis and Kraglin were there, too. Even Nebula stood nearby, observing. When it was all arranged, Peter felt like he should say something, so he told a story:

"I told Gamora how when I was a kid I used to

pretend someone else was my dad," Peter began. "He's a singer and actor from Earth, really famous guy. Yondu didn't have a talking car, but he did have a flying arrow. He didn't have the beautiful voice of an angel, but he did have the whistle of one. Yondu went on adventures and fought robots. I guess *that* guy did kinda end up being my dad after all, only it was you, Yondu." He started to tear up, and paused long enough to get his voice back under control.

"I had a pretty cool dad. What I'm trying to say here is…sometimes, that thing you're searching for your whole life is right there by your side all along, and you don't even know it." Peter paused and looked around the room.

That was all he could say. "I am Groot," Groot said softly.

Rocket nodded. "He did call you 'twig.'"

Nebula walked away from the group. She had only stayed out of respect for Yondu's courage. Now it was time for her to go…but Gamora had one more thing to say to her. She caught up with her sister near a small ship in the Third Quadrant's launch bay.

"I was a child like you," Gamora said. "I was concerned with staying alive until the next day, every day, and I never considered what Thanos was doing to you. I'm trying to make it right. There are little girls like you across the universe who are in danger. You can stay with us and help them."

Nebula thought about it, but only briefly. "I will help them by killing Thanos."

"I don't know if that's possible."

Nebula turned to go. Gamora reached out and caught her arm. Nebula spun, fist raised to strike, but Gamora just stood there, arms open. Slowly, she gathered her sister in for an embrace. Nebula let it happen, and Gamora felt her relax, ever so slightly.

"You will always be my sister," she said quietly.

Nebula raised one arm and laid a hand between Gamora's shoulder blades. They stayed like that for a moment, and then Nebula stepped back and walked away to her ship.

Gamora watched her go before returning to the rest of the group.

When Yondu's pallet was fed into a furnace, his ashes

began to sparkle out into space. The Guardians of the Galaxy watched solemnly, feeling bound together by the experiences they had shared.

"Peter," Kraglin said. "The cap'n found this in a junker shop; said you'd come back to the fold someday." He handed Peter a small electronic device.

Peter took it. It was palm-sized and shiny, with a digital screen. "What is it?"

"It's what everybody's listening to on Earth nowadays. It's got three hundred songs on it."

"Three...hundred songs?" Peter couldn't believe it. That was, like, twenty Awesome Mixes. "Wait," he said as Kraglin turned to go. Kraglin stopped and Peter handed him Yondu's arrow. "Rocket grabbed the pieces and reassembled it. I think Yondu would want you to have it."

"Thanks, Cap'n." Kraglin's voice broke with emotion.

Yondu's ashes sparkled in the void. Beyond them, other lights began to flash.

"They came," Rocket said.

"What is it?" Drax asked.

"I sent word to Yondu's old Ravager buddies," Rocket said. More Ravager ships filled the space near the Third

Quadrant. They had come to pay their respects. Stakar Ogord had lifted Yondu's exile after learning the truth about what he'd done. Every clan had come to salute the Ravager who had helped the Guardians of the Galaxy defeat Ego. Each ship launched special fireworks to commemorate their brother-in-arms in a huge salute across the sky.

"He didn't chase them away," Rocket said.

"No," Peter agreed.

"Even though he yelled at him. And was always mean. And stole batteries he didn't need." Rocket rarely got emotional, but he was kind of a wreck now. All of them were. They had saved the universe, but lost a friend they hadn't known was a friend. Peter and Rocket looked at each other, knowing exactly what Rocket wanted to, but wouldn't, say.

Being a hero was hard sometimes.

Groot crawled from Gamora to Drax and fell asleep on Drax's shoulder. It was always surprising how tender Drax could be.

Peter and Gamora exchanged a look. "What?" he asked.

"It's just…it's an unspoken thing."

He nodded. They moved closer together. The Ravager salute boomed and glittered in the deep void. Mantis and Drax stood close together, too. "It's beautiful," Mantis said.

Drax nodded. "Yes. And so are you." After a moment he added, "On the inside."

The Guardians of the Galaxy looked out into the vast space they had saved, and watched the memorial for their friend.

It was good to be among family.

EPILOGUE

Ayesha's handmaiden approached her nervously. The high priestess was unkempt and distracted. Ever since the Guardians of the Galaxy had escaped her, she had spent days and nights in the laboratory, forbidding access to any other Sovereign nobles. But the handmaiden had her orders, so she dared to approach. "High Priestess. The council is waiting."

"They have determined I have wasted our resources," Ayesha said. "When they see what I have created here, their wrath will dissipate."

The handmaiden looked at the creation. She had never seen anything like it, but it resembled…"It's a new type of birthing pod, ma'am?"

The pod was a ten-foot-tall golden capsule, glowing softly from within, surrounded by curving spikes that focused the energies of creation on what was now growing inside.

"That, my child, is the next step in our evolution," Ayesha said. "More powerful. More beautiful. More capable of destroying the Guardians of the Galaxy." She considered that, relishing the idea of the Guardians' destruction. "I think I shall call him…Adam."

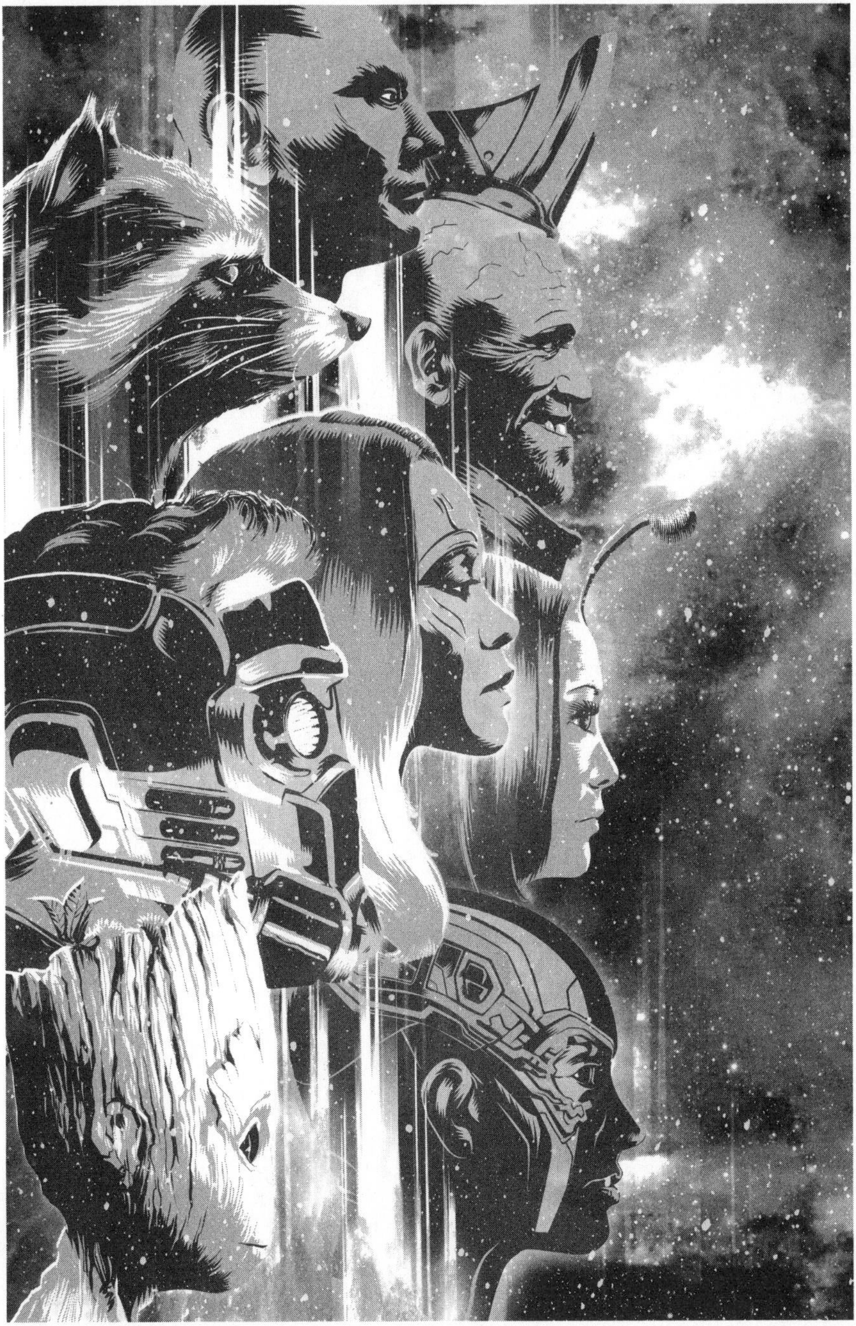

You've seen the Guardians of the Galaxy save the universe again.

Now read how they came together for the first time.

Turn the page for a look at:

It was a great day at the mall. The Xandarian sun was shining, the air was warm, and people were out having a good time. There were families playing, shoppers scoring deals, friends dining outside at the mall's many fine restaurants—and Rocket had nothing but scorn for all of it.

"Xandarians," he grumbled. He surveyed the crowds through a scope, doing a face scan and comparing everyone he saw to a database of outstanding bounties. Only certain people knew about that database, and Rocket was one of them. He liked bounty hunting. It had lots of variety, there was lots of shooting, and the money was tip-top.

He hid in the bushes at the edge of a balcony overlooking the swanky mall plaza below. You could find people with bounties on their heads anywhere, but the high-value marks had a tendency to try to blend in with fancy surroundings. If you wanted to load up on five-hundred-unit lowlifes, there were places for that, but those guys weren't worth Rocket's time. He and Groot were after the big score.

He stood up on tiptoes to get a better look at the areas right below him. Rocket was barely three feet tall, and looked like a cute and cuddly mammal, like you might find begging for treats in a Xandarian family's kitchen. Except as far as he knew there was nothing like him anywhere in the galaxy, and he was not cuddly. No, sir. Rocket liked flying ships real fast, and shooting guns real loud, and breaking any law he ran across.

"What a bunch of losers. All of 'em, in a big hurry to get from stupid to nothing at all. Pathetic," said Rocket, his upper lip curling in disgust.

His scope landed on an average-looking human, strolling by himself. "Look at this guy! You believe they call us criminals when he's assaulting us with that haircut?"

Groot didn't answer, but then, Groot didn't talk much. He was an eight-foot-tall walking tree, more or less, so talking wasn't his strong suit. What Groot was good at was fighting and growing pieces of himself back when they got blown off. Plus he was as strong as any living being Rocket had ever known, which came in handy given Rocket's own compact stature.

Next, Rocket scoped a tiny human stumbling along the sidewalk holding the hands of an adult. "What is this thing? It thinks it's so cool. It's not cool to get help! Walk by yourself, you little gargoyle."

He moved on to an older human, clearly trying to get the interest of a much younger female. "Look at Mr. Smiles over here. Where's your wife, old man? Ha! Right, Groot?"

Rocket laughed, getting a kick out of himself. He turned to see if Groot had seen the old guy, and noticed that Groot wasn't paying attention at all. He was leaning over a nearby fountain and watering his insides. In other words, drinking.

"Don't drink fountain water, you idiot! That's disgusting!" Rocket shouted.

Groot stood up and shook his head, grunting.

"Yes, you did! I just saw you doing it. Why are you lying?"

His scope's alarm went off, notifying Rocket that he'd accidentally waved it so that it focused on someone carrying a bounty. "Oh, looks like we got one," he said. He looked at the target. "Okay, humie," he said. That was his preferred insulting term for humans. "How bad does someone want to find you?"

The display on the scope identified the humie in question as Peter Quill...and the bounty as more than Rocket would have expected. A lot more. "Forty thousand units? Groot, we're gonna be rich."

He turned to see Groot drinking from the fountain again, completely oblivious to this huge potential score. Rocket sighed. Some people.

Peter walked from the mall's main thoroughfare up to the Broker's pawnshop. There was no sign, but the door knew Peter from a previous visit and opened automatically at his approach. The Broker had very good security, and he needed it. He dealt with items that were highly sought after.

"Mr. Quill," the Broker said when he saw Peter enter. He was a smallish humanoid, with ridges on his bare scalp. Hair grew between them but nowhere else on his head except for his eyebrows, which were like small wings swooping over his forehead. He was dressed, as always, in a suit that cost more than all of the clothes Peter had bought in his whole life. Total.

"Broker," Peter said. Getting down to business, he plunked the Orb down on the Broker's desk. "The Orb. As commissioned."

The Broker regarded him with suspicion. "Where is Yondu?"

"Wanted to be here," Peter said. "Sends his love, and told me to tell you that you got the best eyebrows in the business."

The Broker sniffed, dismissing the humorous compliment. He picked up the Orb and set it aside. "What is it?" Peter asked.

"It's my policy never to discuss my clients, or their needs," the Broker said.

"Yeah, well, I almost died getting it for you."

Unfazed, the Broker said, "An occupational hazard, I'm sure, in your line of work."

"Some machine-headed freak," Peter said, describing Korath as he continued his story, "working for a dude named Ronan."

The name had a startling effect on the Broker. "Ronan?" Immediately he came around his desk and began ushering

Peter toward the door. "I'm sorry, Mr. Quill, I truly am, but I want no part of this transaction if Ronan is involved!" He slapped the Orb back into Peter's hands.

"Whoa, whoa! Who's Ronan?" Peter asked. The Broker kept pushing him toward the door.

"A Kree fanatic, outraged by the peace treaty, who will not rest until Xandarian culture—my culture!—is wiped from existence!" He had pushed Peter most of the way to the door by now.

"Come on," Peter said.

"He's someone whose bad side I'd rather not be on," the Broker said. Clearly he was terrified of this Ronan, and Peter couldn't figure it out. He'd never heard of the guy.

"What about my bad side?" he joked, trying to lighten things up a little.

"Farewell, Mr. Quill!" the Broker shouted. He waved to open his door and shoved Peter out.

The moment Peter's body crossed the threshold, the door hissed shut. "Hey, we had a deal, bro!" Peter shouted through the door.

No answer.

He stood there fuming. How was he going to get rich now? Yondu was after him, this Ronan guy seemed like bad news...man, everything was getting complicated.

To one side of the door, a beautiful woman with green skin and long dark hair reddened at the tips was delicately eating a piece of fruit. She was looking at Peter, so he tried to get himself together. He didn't like losing his temper in front of good-looking women.

"What happened?" she asked.

"This guy just backed out of a deal on me," Peter groused. "If there's one thing I hate, it's a man without integrity."

She watched, finishing her fruit. She looked mighty fine in her black leather jumpsuit, and the knives on her hips gave her a nice little air of menace. "Peter Quill," Peter said, introducing himself. "People call me Star-Lord."

"You have the bearing of a man of honor," she said.

"Well, you know, I wouldn't say that," said Peter, playing humble. "People say it about me, but it's not something I would ever say about myself."

As he finished the sentence, she was walking closer to him, and he was enjoying her walking closer to him. Then, almost faster than he could follow, she snatched the Orb from his hands, doubled him over with a kick to the stomach, and ran.

Peter stood up, out of breath. There was no way he would catch her in a footrace. She was fast. Luckily he had a little electronic bolo in his pocket that he kept for circumstances like this one. He activated it and slung it sidearm after her.

The bolo spun through the air past startled shoppers and wrapped itself several times around the woman's knees, bringing her down.

Peter was on her in a second, running and leaping to get hold of her before she could untangle the bolo and get away again. She met him in midair with both feet, kicking him hard off to the side. He hit the pavement, the wind knocked out of him for the second time in fifteen seconds. Before he could get up, she was pounding him with fists, elbows, and feet—all without getting up herself! Even though he was getting beaten senseless, Peter couldn't help but admire her technique.

She straddled him, a look of regret on her face. "This wasn't the plan," she said, and drew one of those knives he'd noticed earlier.

But before she could use it, a tiny ball of fur came flying out of nowhere and knocked her over sideways. She cried out as she hit the pavement and Peter saw what looked like—no, it couldn't be...

It was. A talking raccoon. Big one, maybe three feet tall.

"Put him in the bag!" the raccoon was shouting. The green woman got back to her feet and tried to pull it off, but it hung on for dear life.

Peter looked around. Put who in the bag? Then he saw the walking tree holding a giant sack. It started extruding roots from its body, wrapping them around the green woman.

"Not her—him!" the raccoon shouted. "Learn genders, man!" He was grappling with the green woman's head, and one of his paws slipped into her mouth. She bit him, hard. "Biting? That's not fair!"

Peter happened to agree—biting was not cool—but he wasn't going to stick around and argue about it. Whoever the raccoon and tree were, whatever was happening, he had a chance to get out. He grabbed the Orb and ran, glancing over his shoulder to track their pursuit.

Screaming in fury, the green woman tore the raccoon free and flung him down into the lower level of the plaza. He slammed into a transparent wall and landed in a heap. Peter turned away to gain speed, and a moment later the Orb was knocked out of his hand with a sharp metallic ping. He looked down and saw it rolling away. He also saw a small throwing knife clattering to the pavement.

She'd thrown a knife at him! But not to kill him. *Interesting*, he thought. *She likes me.*

But she seemed to like the Orb more. She jumped over the balcony and ran for the Orb. Peter ran along the balcony as she picked up the Orb, waiting for the right time...now!

He vaulted over and landed on her, driving her to the ground. But she was a lot quicker than he was, and stronger, too. In a moment she had him flipped on his back with one knee pressed hard under his chin.

"Fool," she said. "You should have learned."

"I don't learn," Peter admitted. "One of my issues."

She gave him a look and, just for a second, forgot to stab him. He took the momentary opportunity to slap one of his boot rockets onto her hip and fire it up.

It shot her away over the plaza to land in a shallow reflecting pool. She skidded all the way across the pool, kicking up a big rooster tail along the way and smashing hard into the wall on the other side. The crowd gasped. They hadn't come to the mall for a show like this.

Peter stood, thinking the show was over...and that's when the tree got the drop on him and stuffed him into a sack.

The job was getting complicated, Rocket thought. He hated complicated jobs.

MORE SHIELD! MORE IRON! MORE MUSCLE! MORE HAMMER!

READ THEM ALL!

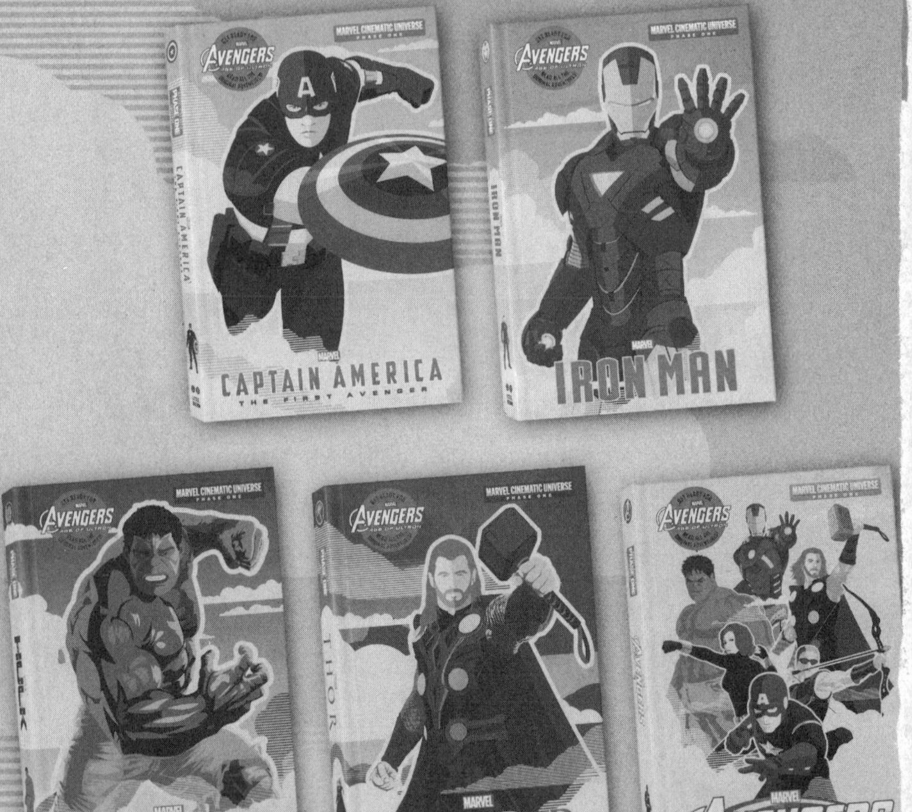
MARVEL CINEMATIC UNIVERSE
PHASE ONE
AVENGERS AGE OF ULTRON
MARVEL
CAPTAIN AMERICA
THE FIRST AVENGER
MARVEL CINEMATIC UNIVERSE
PHASE ONE
AVENGERS AGE OF ULTRON
MARVEL
IRON MAN
MARVEL CINEMATIC UNIVERSE
PHASE ONE
AVENGERS AGE OF ULTRON
MARVEL
THE INCREDIBLE HULK
MARVEL CINEMATIC UNIVERSE
PHASE ONE
AVENGERS AGE OF ULTRON
MARVEL
THOR
MARVEL CINEMATIC UNIVERSE
PHASE ONE
AVENGERS AGE OF ULTRON
MARVEL
THE AVENGERS